Maigret at the
Gai-Moulin

Georges Simenon

Maigret at the Gai-Moulin

Translated by Geoffrey Sainsbury

A Helen and Kurt Wolff Book

Harcourt Brace Jovanovich, Publishers

New York   San Diego   London

Requests for permission to make copies of any part of the work
should be mailed to: Permissions Department, 8th Floor,
Harcourt Brace Jovanovich, Publishers, Orlando, Florida 32887.

At the Gai-Moulin copyright 1940
by Harcourt Brace Jovanovich, Inc.
Copyright renewed 1968
by Harcourt Brace Jovanovich, Inc.
This is a translation of *La Danseuse du Gai-Moulin*, 1931.

Library of Congress Cataloging-in-Publication Data
Simenon, Georges, 1903–1989
[Danseuse du Gai-Moulin.   English]
Maigret at the Gai-Moulin/Georges Simenon: translated
by Geoffrey Sainsbury.—2nd ed.
p.   cm.
Translation of: La danseuse du Gai-Moulin.
ISBN 0-15-155568-0
I. Title.
PQ2637.I53D313   1991   91-7774
843'.912—dc20

Printed in the United States of America
Second edition
A B C D E

Maigret at the
Gai-Moulin

—1—

The Foreigner

"Who is he?"

"I don't know," said Adèle, after blowing out a cloud of cigarette smoke. "I never saw him here before."

Lazily she uncrossed her legs, patted her hair to make sure it was in place, and examined her makeup in one of the mirrors with which the room was lined.

She was sitting on one of the crimson plush seats, with a young man on either side of her. On the table in front of them were three glasses of port.

"You don't mind, do you?"

She gave a friendly, confiding smile to her companions as she stood up. With a slight roll of her hips, she walked over to the newcomer.

The proprietor gave a nod to the orchestra, and its four members sang a verse of the tune they were playing. There was only one couple on the floor, who danced because they were paid to.

It was like that every night. The place seemed deserted. The room was too large for the few people who came, and the mirrors all around made it seem larger still, with their endless reflections of crimson plush seats and gray-white marble tables.

The two young men—really boys—shifted closer to one another, filling the gap Adèle had left.

"She's charming." Jean Chabot, the younger, sighed. With a poise that was assumed, he looked around the room with half-closed eyes.

"Hot stuff!" said his friend, René Delfosse, whose hands were folded over the gold knob of his walking stick.

Chabot was between sixteen and seventeen; Delfosse was eighteen at the most. The latter was a weedy, unhealthy-looking boy with poor features. Young as they were, they would both have been indignant at any suggestion that they were unversed in the ways of the world—particularly the bad ways.

"Here! Victor!" Chabot adopted a familiar tone in speaking to the passing waiter. "Do you know who he is?"

"No. But he's ordered champagne."

And with a wink Victor went on:

"Adèle will look after him."

He moved off with his tray. The orchestra stopped, then struck up again with a tango. The proprietor himself was uncorking the newcomer's champagne, having wound a napkin around the neck of the bottle.

"Do you think they'll be shutting late?" whispered Chabot.

"Between two and half past . . . As usual."

"Shall we have another drink?"

They were nervous, particularly the younger one, who stared from face to face with uneasy eyes.

"How much do you think there'll be in it?"

Delfosse shrugged, and snapped impatiently: "Shut up!"

Adèle and her customer were sitting almost opposite them. He was a man about forty, with black hair and a dull, sallow complexion. A Romanian, a Turk, or something of that kind. He wore a pink silk shirt, and a diamond glittered in his tie.

He took little notice of Adèle as she talked and laughed and leaned on his shoulder. When she asked him for a cigarette, he produced a gold cigarette case and looked straight in front of him as he handed it to her.

Delfosse and Chabot were silent. They did their best to look at the foreigner with disdain, but actually they admired him intensely. No detail escaped them. They studied his tie and the cut of his suit, and followed every movement as he lifted his glass of champagne.

Chabot's suit was ready-made, and his shoes had been resoled more than once. His friend's clothes, though of better material, fit badly. Or perhaps it was the fault of his figure. His shoulders were too narrow.

"Here comes another customer."

The plush curtain that hung across the entrance had been pulled aside. A man appeared and stood looking around the room. He was massive, his face placid. He ignored the waiter who started to lead him to a table. Strolling into the room, he sat down at the first one he came to.

"Do you have any beer?"

"Only English beer. Pale Ale . . . Stout . . ."

The man waved a hand, as though it didn't matter.

So there was no more happening than on most evenings. It was a lifeless *boîte de nuit* in a provincial town. A nightclub, you might call it, except that it wasn't a club. There was a solitary couple dancing; jazz that no one listened to, providing a background; an overdressed customer at the bar, throwing dice with Génaro, the proprietor. And there was Adèle and the man she was sitting with, who still took no notice of her.

At one point, three men who were slightly drunk emerged from the folds of the curtain. The proprietor rushed toward them, and the orchestra did its best. But in vain. They charged out, laughing scornfully as they went.

Time dragged on, and Chabot and Delfosse became quieter and quieter. Fatigue drew lines on their faces, hollowed their eyes, and took all the freshness from their complexions, painting them a nasty leaden color.

"Do you really think . . ." began Chabot, but so low that the other guessed the words rather than heard them.

No answer. Delfosse merely drummed his fingers on the marble table.

Leaning against the foreigner, Adèle winked now and then at the two boys, but without ever dropping her mask of playful affection.

"Victor!"

4

"Going so early?"

Delfosse's tone was tense and enigmatic as he answered:

"We'll settle tomorrow. We came without any money."

"All right, messieurs! . . . Good night, messieurs! . . . Are you going out that way?"

The boys were not drunk, but they left in a sort of trance, seeing nothing.

There were two doors to the Gai-Moulin. The front one, used by customers, opened onto Rue du Pot d'Or. But after two in the morning, when, according to regulations, the place should be closed, any customers who stayed on were let out through the back door, beyond the lavatory, a door that opened onto a narrow badly lighted alley.

Chabot and Delfosse entered the lavatory, where they stood for a moment without looking at one another.

"I'm scared . . ." stammered Chabot.

He looked at himself in the oval mirror. The muffled sound of jazz had followed them.

"Quick!" said Delfosse, opening a door and disclosing a dark flight of brick steps, from which rose a damp chill. The steps led down to the cellar, which reeked of beer and wine.

"Suppose someone comes!"

The door shut behind them, blotting out all light. In the pitch blackness Chabot nearly fell. His hands felt for the wall, which was covered with mold. Someone touched him, and he jumped back, but it was only his friend, who growled:

"Keep still."

5

The music was almost inaudible now—only a faint, rhythmic throb, accentuated now and then by the thud of the drums. It was enough, however, to evoke the scene they had left: the crimson plush seats, the couple who never stopped dancing.

It was cold. Chabot could feel the dampness going right through him, and the back of his neck was icy. He had to stifle a sneeze. Delfosse's breathing was loud, and each breath wafted tobacco toward him.

Someone entered the lavatory. They could hear the water running. A tip was thrown into the saucer.

The ticking of Delfosse's watch could be heard too.

"Do you think we'll be able to open it?" Chabot asked.

Delfosse gripped his hand to make him shut up. His fingers were cold.

Upstairs, the proprietor was no doubt beginning to look impatiently at the clock. If they happened to have a good night, he was quite ready to risk a raid and stay open after hours. But when the place was almost empty, he respected the regulations.

"Two o'clock, gentlemen! . . . Closing time! . . ."

The boys on the steps could not hear him, but they could guess, minute by minute, all that was going on: the customers paying their bills, then Victor going to the bar to settle with the proprietor, who was at the till. Meanwhile, the musicians would be packing their instruments and putting the bass drum into its loose green cover. The other waiter, Joseph, would be clearing the tables and stacking the chairs on them.

"Closing time! Come on, Adèle; hurry up!"

The proprietor was a short, thickset Italian, who

had worked in bars and hotels in Cannes, Nice, Biarritz, and Paris.

Steps crossed the lavatory—someone locking the back door. He turned the key in the lock, but did not withdraw it. A bolt was shot.

Would he lock the cellar door too? Or open the door and glance down the steps? There was a pause. Perhaps he was looking in the mirror to make sure his hair was neat. He coughed. Then a door creaked, and he went back into the main room.

In five minutes the place would be empty of customers. The Italian would pull down the shutters in front. After that, he'd wait for the last of the staff to go. Then he'd lock up and leave too.

He never took all the money with him. If there was a thousand-franc note, he would slip it in his pocket, but the rest would be left in the drawer under the bar, whose lock was not strong enough to stand up to a good knife.

The lights would by now be going out, one after the other. . . .

"Come on!" Delfosse said.

"Not yet . . . Wait a little longer."

They were alone in the place, yet they still spoke in a whisper. And their being invisible to one another did not prevent them from knowing that their features were drawn, their faces pale.

"Suppose someone stayed behind . . ."

"My courage didn't fail when I went through my father's safe, did it?" Delfosse spoke in a snarl.

"There might be nothing in the till."

Chabot felt dizzy, as if he were drunk. He couldn't bear the idea of leaving the cellar. He was on the verge of collapsing on the steps and sobbing. Again Delfosse said:

"Come on!"

"Wait! He might come back to get something."

They waited five minutes, then another five, Chabot finding every pretext for delay. His shoelace had come untied, and he must tie it, so he wouldn't trip and make a noise. He fumbled with it in the dark as long as he could.

"I thought you had more guts than this. Come on! Get going!"

Delfosse meant Chabot to go first. He pushed him forward with trembling hands. The cellar door opened. A faucet dripped in a sink. There was a smell of soap and disinfectant.

Chabot knew very well that the door to the main room would creak. He braced himself for the dreaded sound; yet he couldn't stop a shiver running down his spine.

A vast emptiness. The room, in the darkness, seemed as big as a cathedral. Warm currents of air still drifted from the radiators.

"Give me a light!" Chabot whispered.

Delfosse struck a match. They paused to take a breath and get their bearings.

Suddenly the match dropped. A piercing shriek came from Delfosse. He made a dash for the lavatory door, missed it in the dark, retraced his steps, and bumped into Chabot.

"Quick! Let's get out!" he said hoarsely.

Chabot too had seen something, though not clearly. . . . Something like a human body stretched out on the floor near the bar . . . A head with black hair . . .

They stood still, trying to pull themselves together. The box of matches had been dropped, and of course they couldn't find it.

"Where are yours?" Delfosse asked.

"I haven't got any."

One of them bumped into a table. The other asked:

"Where are you?"

"This way! I found the door."

The faucet was still dripping—a reassuring sound. They were halfway to safety.

"Should we switch on the light?"

"Are you crazy?"

Hands groped. The door was unlocked. Hands groped again, this time for the bolt.

"It's stiff."

Steps sounded in the alley outside. They held their breath and waited. A scrap of a sentence:

"To my mind, if only England hadn't . . ."

The voice faded away. Two policemen, perhaps, talking politics.

"Why don't you open it?"

But Delfosse couldn't. He was leaning against the door with both hands pressed to his heaving chest.

"He had . . . his mouth open . . ." he stammered.

With an effort, he turned and opened the door. At last they were outside. Their legs ached to run. Neither thought of shutting the door behind them.

At the end of the alley was Rue du Pont d'Avroy, which was well lighted and, in spite of the late hour, not altogether deserted. They walked as slowly as they could, without looking at each other. Chabot felt utterly empty, numb, as if he were moving through a world of cotton wool. The sounds that reached him seemed to come from very far away.

"Do you think he's dead? . . . It was the Turk, wasn't it?"

"Yes. It was him all right . . . His mouth was open. And one eye . . ."

"What do you mean?"

"One eye was shut, but the other was open . . . I'm thirsty."

All the cafés on Rue du Pont d'Avroy were closed. The only place open was a little bar where you could get beer, mussels, pickled herring, and fried potatoes.

"Let's try it."

The cook, all in white, poked up the fire. A woman eating in a corner greeted the boys with an engaging smile.

"Two glasses of beer . . . and some fried potatoes. And, yes, mussels too."

When they had eaten that, they ordered the same again. They were ravenous. And they had four glasses of beer each.

Each was intent on his plate, and avoided looking at the other. Outside, in the darkness, an occasional person hurried by on his way home.

"The check, please!"

An awful moment of anxiety followed. They'd forgotten about money. Would they have enough? It was all very well at the Gai-Moulin to say they'd left their money at home. They couldn't do that here.

"Seven and two fifty and three and . . . Eighteen seventy-five."

There was just one franc left for the tip.

On the street, shuttered shop fronts and lines of street lights. The distant sound of a police patrol doing its rounds. The boys crossed the Meuse.

Delfosse said nothing, but stared rigidly in front of him. His mind was so far away, he hardly knew his friend was speaking to him.

Chabot, dreading the moment when he would be left alone, saw Delfosse all the way home to his substantial house in the best part of town. When they reached it, he said imploringly:

"Don't go in yet. Come partway with me. . . ."

"No! I feel rotten."

It was the right word. They felt rotten, both of them. Chabot had barely seen the body, but his imagination had been busily detailing that vague figure on the floor.

"You're really sure it was the Turk?"

They were calling him the Turk for want of any better name.

Delfosse didn't answer. He put his key in the lock, and the door opened on a large dark hall, in which the only thing visible was a brass umbrella stand.

"See you tomorrow!"

"At the Pelican?"

The door was already closing. Chabot felt the ground sinking beneath his feet. If only he was home, in bed! Wouldn't that bring this nightmare to an end?

But there he was, all alone on the empty street. He walked faster and faster, then started running. At each corner he hesitated, then dashed on again as if possessed. In the Place du Congrès he steered clear of the trees. Hearing steps in the distance, he slowed down, but whoever it was was going in another direction.

Rue de la Loi. Two-story houses. A front door.

Jean Chabot took out his key and let himself in. Turning on the light in the hall, he went past the glass-paneled door into the kitchen, where the fire was still glowing faintly. He returned to shut the front door, which he had forgotten. It was hot and stuffy in the kitchen. On the table, which was covered with white oilcloth, he saw a penciled note from his father:

You'll find a cutlet in the icebox and a piece of pie. Good night.

In the light, Jean looked stunned. He opened the icebox, but the sight of the cutlet made him feel sick.

On the windowsill was a plant in a pot—something like groundsel in more ambitious form. That meant that Aunt Marie had been to see them. She never came without bringing a plant of some kind, which she gave with copious instructions about how it should be cared for. Her own house, on Quai Saint-Léonard, had plants in every room.

Jean switched off the lights and crept upstairs in his socks. On the second floor were the bedrooms they rented. Above were the attic rooms in which the family slept. The cold filtered through the roof.

When he reached the top of the stairs, the springs of a bed creaked. Someone had waked up—his father

12

or his mother. As quietly as he could, he opened the door of his own room.

But a muffled voice reached him:

"Is that you, Jean?"

Hell! He had to go and say good night. The atmosphere in his parents' room was moist and sleepy. They'd been in bed for hours.

"Isn't it very late?"

"Not very."

"You ought . . ."

But his father couldn't bring himself to scold him. Or perhaps he felt it would be useless.

"Good night, my boy."

Jean bent over and placed a kiss on the warm, damp forehead.

"You're frozen. . . . You . . ."

"It's cold outdoors."

"Did you find the cutlet? . . . Aunt Marie brought the pie."

"I had a snack with my friend."

His mother turned in her sleep, her hair spreading over the pillow.

"Good night!"

He couldn't stand anything more. Alone in his room, he didn't even switch the light on. Throwing his jacket on the floor, he flung himself on his bed and buried his face in the pillow.

There were no tears. He couldn't find any. But he panted, and every limb trembled. His whole body, in fact, was seized by a fit of shivering, as though he was coming down with some serious illness.

His main thought was not to let the bedsprings creak. And he had to suppress the spasm that was gripping his throat. For he knew his father would be lying awake in the next room, listening.

One image filled his mind, growing bigger and bigger; one name thundered in his ears, louder and louder:

"The Turk."

It crushed him, suffocated him. He writhed under the weight of it.

For hours . . .

And, suddenly, there was the sun streaming through the little skylight, and there was his father standing at the foot of the bed, saying in a coaxing voice:

"You can't go on like this, Jean. . . . You've been drinking again, haven't you? You didn't even undress."

From downstairs rose the odor of eggs and bacon and coffee. Trucks rattled down the street. Doors slammed. A cock crowed.

−2−

Petty Cash

Jean pushed his plate away, put his elbows on the table, and stared through the muslin curtains into the little sunlit whitewashed yard.

His father, as he ate his breakfast, watched him out of the corner of his eye. He made an effort at conversation.

"Do you know if it's true that the big apartment building on Rue Féronstrée is going to be put up for sale? Someone asked me yesterday at the office. Perhaps you ought to inquire, Jean."

Madame Chabot too was examining her son as she peeled the onions for the soup. The subject of buildings went no further, because she now cut in:

"So you can't eat your breakfast?"

"I'm not hungry, Maman."

"And I know why! You were drunk again last night, weren't you?"

"No."

"Do you think I can't see it? With those red eyes, and your face the color of putty? A lot of good it is, trying to feed you. Come! You could at least eat the eggs."

But he couldn't have eaten them even for a fortune. He had a tight feeling in his chest. Everything churned his stomach: the smell of the bacon, and of the soup that was just coming to a boil; even the quiet homeliness of the kitchen and the white wall outside made him nauseous.

He longed to get away. And, above all, to *know.* He quailed at the least sound from outside.

"I've got to be going."

"You have plenty of time. . . . You were with Delfosse last night, weren't you? If I catch him coming here again to get you . . . A boy who loafs around doing nothing, just because his father's rich . . . It's all very well for him: he doesn't have to get up in the morning and go to work. But you do! . . . Besides, he's depraved."

Monsieur Chabot said nothing, but looked down at his plate. He didn't want to take sides. One of the roomers came downstairs and went straight out the front door. He was a Polish student, off to the university. Another roomer could be heard moving in the room over the kitchen.

"This kind of thing leads to a bad end, Jean. You'll see! Ask your father if he carried on like that at your age!"

The boy's eyes really were bloodshot, and his features were drawn. His forehead had blotches.

"I really have to go," he repeated, glancing at the clock.

As he spoke, someone rattled the mailbox by the door. It was the signal given by friends; the bell served for more formal visitors. Jean rushed to open the door and found himself face to face with René Delfosse, who asked:

"Are you coming?"

"Yes. I'll be right with you."

"Come in, Delfosse!" Madame Chabot called out from the kitchen. "I was just saying to Jean that it was time to put a stop to these goings-on. They're ruining his health. If you ruin yours, it's your business—and your parents—but Jean . . ."

With an embarrassed smile, René hung his head. He was tall and thin, and his face was even paler than Jean's.

"Jean has to earn his living. *We* aren't rich people. You should have sense enough to understand that. So I must ask you to leave him out of what you do."

"Come on!" whispered Jean, who could hardly stand this.

"I assure you, madame . . . we . . ." René faltered.

"What time did *you* get home last night?"

"I'm not quite sure. Somewhere around one."

"Jean's admitted it was well past two!"

"Really, Maman, I must be off."

Jean dragged his friend out of the house. As soon as they'd gone, Monsieur Chabot went into the hall and put his things on too.

Outside, as in all the streets of Liège at that hour of the morning, housewives with pails of water were

17

sluicing down their small front sidewalks. Wagons and carts with vegetables and coal were drawn up here and there by the curb, and street cries echoed.

"Well?"

Having turned the corner, the two boys could voice their anxieties.

"Nothing! There's not a word about it in the morning papers. Perhaps they haven't found him yet."

René wore a student cap with a long visor, like that worn by many of the hundreds of students making their way to the university. They formed a kind of procession over the bridge across the Meuse.

"My mother's furious with me. And even more with you."

They crossed the market, treading on cabbage and lettuce leaves. Jean stared straight in front of him.

"And what about the money? It's the fifteenth," he said.

They crossed to the other side of the street, to avoid passing the door of a certain tobacconist, to whom they owed fifty francs.

"I haven't forgotten. This morning I looked in my father's wallet, but there were only big notes in it."

Lowering his voice, René went on:

"Don't worry. I'll go to my uncle's on Rue Léopold. There's a ten-to-one chance of my being left alone in the shop for a minute or two."

Jean knew the place—the most important chocolate shop in Liège. He could picture his friend slipping his hand in the till.

"When will I see you?"

"I'll wait for you at lunchtime."

They reached the office of the notary Lhoest, who

was Jean's employer. As they shook hands, without looking at each other, Jean had an uncomfortable feeling, as if his friend's handshake was not quite the same as usual.

But yes, everything was different now. They were accomplices now.

Jean's desk was in the hall. As junior clerk, his job was to stamp envelopes, sort incoming letters, and run errands.

This morning he bent silently over his work, making himself as small as possible and not looking at anyone who passed. That's not to say he didn't see them. He noticed everyone who passed him, and was particularly conscious of the movements of the chief clerk, a stern-looking man of fifty, from whom he got his orders.

Eleven o'clock passed, and everything seemed to be going smoothly. But just before twelve, the chief clerk approached him.

"Have you done the petty-cash account, Chabot?"

All morning Jean had been rehearsing his answer. He brought it out now, with his eyes averted.

"Excuse me, Monsieur Hosay, but I put on a different suit this morning. The account book and the money are in the one I wore yesterday. I'll get them during lunch hour. . . ."

He was so pale that the chief clerk, looking surprised, asked:

"Are you ill?"

"No . . . At least, I don't know . . . maybe a little . . ."

The petty cash was Jean's responsibility. Twice a

month, on the fifteenth and at the end, he was given a sum of money, and at the same time he had to produce the little account book in which the last fortnight's expenses for stamps, fares, and so on was entered.

The office emptied for lunch hour. As soon as he was in the street, the junior clerk looked for René. He spied him standing outside the tobacconist's, smoking a gold-tipped cigarette.

"Well?"

"Come! . . . It's all right."

They walked quickly. They needed to feel the crowd jostling them.

"Let's go to the Pelican. . . . I went to my uncle's. I had only a few seconds to dive in the till and grab what I could. . . . I took too much."

"How much?"

"Almost two thousand francs."

Jean was aghast.

"Here, take three hundred for the petty cash. We'll go fifty-fifty in the rest."

"No."

There was a threatening note in the way René insisted. "Of course we will. Don't we always go fifty-fifty?"

"I don't want all that money."

"Nor do I."

They looked up automatically at the stone balcony of a second-floor window. Behind that window was the furnished room occupied by Adèle, the Gai-Moulin dancer.

"You haven't been back there?"

"I went along Rue du Pot d'Or. The doors were open, and Victor and Joseph were sweeping the place out—just like any other morning."

Jean was wringing his hands so tightly he almost bruised his knuckles.

"But there was no doubt about it, was there? You're sure . . . ?"

"I'm sure it was the Turk," snapped René, then shuddered.

"When you went back, there weren't police in the street?"

"Not a sign of anything unusual. Victor caught sight of me and shouted good morning."

They went into the Pelican, sat at a table near the door, and ordered English beer. They had hardly done this when Jean's attention was caught by a customer sitting almost opposite him.

"Don't look around; look in the mirror . . . He was there last night. Do you remember?"

"The bulky fellow? . . . Yes, that's right."

He had been the last arrival, the evening before, at the Gai-Moulin, the powerful, broad-shouldered man who had asked for beer.

"Looks like a stranger here."

"Yes. And he's smoking French tobacco. Be careful! He's looking at us."

"Waiter!" called René. "How much do we owe you? . . . Forty-two francs, isn't it?"

He produced his wallet and fished out a hundred-franc note, showing several others as he did so.

"Here! Keep the change."

They weren't able to keep still. They had been

sitting only a minute or two, and now they were off again. As they walked away, Jean couldn't help looking around anxiously.

"The man's following us! At least, he's behind us."

"Shut up! You'll give me a heart attack. What would he be following us for?"

"They must have found the Turk. Unless he wasn't dead, after all. Do you think . . . ?"

"Oh, shut up, will you!"

René spoke with increasing sharpness.

They walked on in silence for three hundred yards or so before Jean asked:

"Do you think we ought to go back again tonight?"

"Of course! It would look fishy otherwise."

"Do you think Adèle knows anything?"

Jean was really on edge. He didn't know what to say or which way to look. He could feel the man's eyes drilling holes in his back, but he didn't dare turn around again.

"If he's still behind us when we cross the bridge, it will mean he's following us for certain."

"Are you going home?"

"I have to. My mother's in a state."

Not half the state he was in himself. He could have burst into tears.

"He's crossing the bridge. . . . You see! I was right."

"Shut up! . . . We'll meet this evening. . . . I'm going this way."

"René!"

"What?"

"I don't want all this money. Listen . . ."

But his friend walked off with a shrug.

Jean quickened his step, looking in shop windows for the reflection of his pursuer.

In the quiet streets on this side of the river, there was no longer any room for doubt. His legs felt weak, but he walked all the quicker, driven along giddily by fear.

At home, his mother asked:

"What on earth's the matter?"

"Nothing."

"Pale's not the word! Why, you're positively green!"

And then she burst out:

"A pretty state of affairs! . . . To get like that at your age . . . Where were you last night? And who were you with, besides Delfosse? . . . I can't understand your father. He's far too lenient with you. . . . Now sit down and eat your lunch."

"I'm not hungry."

"What? Again?"

"Please, Maman, please! I'm feeling rotten. I don't know what's the matter with me."

But Madame Chabot's sharp eye did not soften. She was a brisk, quick-tempered woman, on the go morning, noon, and night.

"If you're ill, I'll call the doctor."

"No. Please . . ."

Steps on the stairs. The head of one of the roomers was visible through the glass-paneled door. He knocked and came in. His expression was worried, mistrustful.

"Do you know the man who's walking up and down outside, Madame Chabot?"

He had a strong Slavic accent and very shiny eyes. An excitable person, who flared up at the least thing, he was past the normal age to be a student, and he never attended lectures, though year after year he was registered at the university.

He was known to be a Georgian and to have dabbled in politics in his own country. He claimed to be an aristocrat.

"What man, Monsieur Bogdanowsky?"

"Have a look."

He led her into the dining room, which looked out on the street. Jean hesitated, but finally went too.

"He's been walking up and down for the last quarter of an hour. It's the police! I know what I'm talking about."

"Ridiculous!" said Madame Chabot. "You have police on the brain. He looks to me as though he's waiting for somebody."

The Georgian was not reassured. With a suspicious look at the man outside, he grumbled something in his own language and returned to his room. But Jean recognized the broad-shouldered man.

"Come and have your lunch. Now! No nonsense, or I'll pack you off to bed and get the doctor."

Monsieur Chabot never came home for lunch. Mother and son ate in the kitchen, with Madame Chabot jumping up from her chair every other minute and moving to and fro between the table and the stove.

She studied Jean with a critical eye as he bent over his plate and made a desperate effort to swallow a few mouthfuls. Suddenly she noticed his tie.

"Well! Another! Where did that one come from?"

"I . . . It was given to me. . . . René . . ."

"René! Always René! I'd have thought you had more pride. I'm ashamed of you. . . . They may be rolling in money, those Delfosses, but that doesn't make them any better. Why, his parents aren't even married. . . ."

"Maman!"

But he said it coaxingly, hoping to touch a soft spot. All he wanted was to be left in peace during the hour he had to be at home. Especially since he could picture the stranger pacing up and down opposite, in front of the school where he had spent his early years.

"No, son! You can take my word for it: you're on the wrong track. You must mend your ways if you don't want to end up like Uncle Philippe."

Uncle Philippe was the black sheep of the family, constantly held up as an example. From time to time he would be seen dead-drunk in the street, or on a ladder painting a house.

"He had as good an education as anyone. He could have made a fine career for himself."

With his mouth full, Jean dashed into the hall, tore his jacket from its peg, and bolted.

In Liège, some papers had a morning edition, but the most important one came out at two in the afternoon. In a cloud, Jean walked toward the center of town—a sunny cloud, which made everything seem hazy around him. It was not until after he had crossed the Meuse that he was jolted out of it by the words:

"*Gazette de Liège! Gazette de Liège!* . . . Corpse found in wicker basket! . . . Gruesome details! . . . *Gazette de Liège!*"

Less than six feet away, the broad-shouldered man bought a copy and stood waiting for his change. Jean felt for some coins, but all he could find were the notes René had given him, which he had simply stuffed into a pocket. Giving up, he walked on, and a few moments later made his way into the lawyer's office. He was the last to arrive.

"Five minutes late!" said the chief clerk. "It's not much, but it happens too frequently."

"I'm sorry. . . . The streetcar . . . I've got the petty cash."

He tried to look natural, but his eyes had a queer glint in them, and he could feel his cheeks burning.

Monsieur Hosay opened the little account book and checked the totals.

"You should have a hundred and eighteen fifty."

Jean cursed himself for not having broken one of the hundred-franc notes. He could hear the assistant clerk discussing the wicker-basket affair with the typist.

"Graphopoulos. What kind of a name is that?"

"Greek. . . ."

The words hummed in Jean's ears. He pulled two notes out of his pocket. Monsieur Hosay looked coldly at something that fell to the floor—a third hundred-franc note.

"You seem to handle money very casually. Don't you have a wallet?"

"I'm sorry."

"If Monsieur Lhoest saw you putting notes straight into your pocket! . . . I don't have any change. Carry the balance forward, and when you've got through that, come to me for more. . . . This afternoon you're to go around to the newspapers with the legal notices.

And look sharp about it! It's very important that they appear tomorrow."

The Turk was a Greek! . . .

Outside, Jean's first thought was to buy a paper. He stood in the center of a chattering group while the man found change for a hundred-franc note. Jean walked off at last, reading, careless of the many people he bumped into.

MYSTERY OF THE WICKER BASKET

Nine o'clock this morning, in the Zoo, one of the keepers discovered a large wicker basket standing in the middle of the lawn.

Imagine his horror when he opened it and found the fully dressed body of a man, in a huddled position, with his head between his knees.

The keeper at once called the police, who in turn reported the matter to the inspector of the Fourth Division. So tightly was the body jammed into the basket that it took considerable force to extricate it.

The man appears to be about forty. His wallet was missing, but some business cards, bearing the name Ephraim Graphopoulos, were found in a pocket.

He is thought to have arrived in Liège recently. His name is not on the list of foreign residents, nor is it on any of the forms that are filled out by every new arrival at a hotel.

The postmortem will be carried out this afternoon. For the moment, all the police will say is that the man died during the night, from wounds that appear to have been inflicted by a heavy, blunt instrument.

In our next edition we hope to be in a position to give further details of this case, which promises to be sensational.

Holding the newspaper in his hand, Jean entered the advertisement office of *La Meuse*, handed in the legal notices, and waited for his receipt.

The town was buzzing with activity in the September sunshine. It would probably be one of the last warm days of autumn. On the boulevards men were sawing and hammering, putting up the stalls for the great October fair.

Jean looked behind him, but there was no sign of his follower. Passing the Pelican, he peeped in to see if René was there, since he knew his friend had no classes that afternoon.

Then he went out of his way to walk along Rue du Pot d'Or. The doors of the Gai-Moulin were open, but it was so dark inside, he could hardly see the crimson plush of the seats. Victor was cleaning the windows. Jean hurried on, not wanting to be noticed. First he went to the *Express*, and next to the *Journal de Liège*.

Adèle's balcony fascinated him. He hesitated. Once before, he had paid her a visit, knocking at her door about midnight, on some futile pretext. She had received him in a grubby dressing gown, and had then gone on dressing in front of him, chattering in the most natural way.

He hadn't attempted to go further. Her casual intimacy had nonetheless made him very happy.

28

René, he'd been to see her too—or said he had. In fact, he swore their meeting had been spent in quite another way.

Jean pushed open the door beside the grocer's shop, climbed the dark stairs, and knocked.

There was no answer. Soon, however, slippered feet could be heard shuffling across the floor. The door opened slightly, and a strong smell of methylated spirit reached his nostrils.

"Oh, it's you! . . . I thought it would be your friend."

"Why?"

Adèle went back toward the little nickel spirit lamp on which she had left her curling iron.

"Shut the door, will you? That draft will blow the lamp out."

Suddenly Jean was seized by a wish to confide in her, to tell her everything. Surely she would be able to give him advice. At any rate she could console him, this woman with tired eyes, whose flesh under her dressing gown no longer had quite the firmness of youth, but was, all the same, very attractive—this woman who dragged her feet, in red satin slippers, back and forth across her untidy room.

On the unmade bed lay a copy of the *Gazette de Liège*.

—3—

The Broad-shouldered Man

Adèle had not been up long. Beside the spirit lamp was a can of condensed milk with a dribble down one side.

"So your friend's not with you?" she asked.

Jean's face clouded, and it was in a sulky voice that he answered:

"Why should he be?"

She opened a drawer and fished out a shrimp-colored chemise.

"Is it true his father's a big manufacturer?"

Jean had not sat down. As he watched her moving around, he was assailed by mixed feelings: dejection, desire, instinctive respect for women, and, last, despair.

She was certainly not beautiful, particularly in those slippers and that grubby dressing gown. But somehow that was all the nicer. He was being admitted into something that lay beneath the surface.

Was she twenty-five or thirty? She had certainly had time to see a good deal of life. She often spoke of Paris, Berlin, and Ostend, and would mention the names of the most celebrated *boîtes de nuit*.

But she spoke of it all without enthusiasm, without bragging, without pretense. Her main trait was lassitude. It was written all over her—in her smile, in her green eyes, in her movements, and in the casual way she held a cigarette between her lips.

A gracious lassitude.

"What does he make?"

"Bicycles."

"How funny! I knew a bicycle manufacturer once. At Saint-Etienne. How old is he?"

"The father?"

"No. René."

He didn't like hearing her call his friend by his Christian name.

"Eighteen."

"A rascal, I bet!"

She spoke with complete familiarity, as to an old pal. They were on equal footing. When she spoke of René, however, there was a hint of deference in her voice.

Had she guessed that the Chabots were not rich people? That they were perhaps no better than the family she had sprung from?

"Sit down. . . . You don't mind if I finish dressing, do you? . . . Hand me the cigarettes. . . ."

He looked around.

"Over there by the bed . . . That's right."

Jean turned paler. He could hardly bring himself to touch the cigarette case. It was the gold one he had seen the night before in the hands of the black-haired foreigner. He looked at Adèle, the whole of whose leg was visible as she dragged on a stocking.

And now he blushed violently. Was it because of the cigarette case? Or that expanse of bare skin? Probably both. The two things somehow went together. She was a woman, but she was more than that. A woman in some way mixed up in a mysterious affair, a woman with a secret.

"What's the matter?"

He pulled himself together and handed her the cigarettes.

"Have you got a light?"

His hand trembled as he held out a lighted match. She burst out laughing.

"You haven't seen many women in your life. It's not hard to tell that!"

"I've had more than one mistress."

She laughed all the louder. Screwing up her eyes, she studied his face.

"You're a funny boy. . . . Toss me my garter belt."

"Did you get home very late last night?"

She looked at him more seriously.

"You don't mean to say you've fallen in love? . . . And jealous too! . . . I begin to understand the look on your face just now, when I mentioned René. Go on! Turn around! Face to the wall, please."

"You haven't seen the papers?"

"I only glanced at mine. Why?"

"The man you were with last night was killed."

"No! You're joking."

She wasn't very excited. Curious; no more.

"Who did it?"

"They don't know. They found his body in a wicker basket."

The dressing gown was thrown on the bed. When Jean turned around, she was getting a dress out of the wardrobe.

"I suppose that'll mean trouble for me. Just my luck . . ."

"You left the Gai-Moulin with him?"

"No."

"Ah!"

"You sound as though you didn't believe me. Do you think I bring every customer home with me? . . . I'm a dancer, my boy. My job is to make people order champagne. But once the place is closed, my day's work is done. Understand?"

"But with René . . ."

"With René what?"

"Nothing . . . But he told me . . ."

"He's a fool. If he's kissed me, that's as far as he's ever gone. . . . Give me another cigarette."

She put on a jacket.

"Come! I have some shopping to do. . . . Shut the door."

He followed her down the dingy staircase.

"Which way do you go?"

"Back to the office."

"You'll be coming tonight?"

They went their separate ways through the crowded streets, and a few minutes later Jean was sitting at his desk, facing a pile of envelopes waiting to be stamped.

33

Without his knowing why, his mood had changed. It was no longer fear, but sadness that had the upper hand. Dejectedly he looked at the walls, which were covered with notices of auction sales.

"You haven't given me the receipts," said the chief clerk.

He handed them over.

"And what about the *Gazette de Liège*? You don't mean to say you've forgotten the *Gazette de Liège*?"

It was serious. A catastrophe, in fact. The chief clerk's voice was positively tragic.

"Listen, Chabot! It's high time you realized that things can't go on like this. Work's work. Duty's duty. I'll have to speak to Monsieur Lhoest about you. You don't seem to take life very seriously. I'm told that you're seen at night in places that are not respectable, places in which even I would not dare set foot. . . . It won't do. . . . And kindly look at me when I speak to you, and take that supercilious grin off your face. Do you hear me? . . . You'd better get hold of yourself. . . ."

With that, the door slammed, and Jean was left alone to stamp the envelopes.

One minute to five. A long minute for Jean as he watched the second hand jerk forward sixty times. Then he stood up, locked the drawer of his desk, and left.

Where would René be? In one of the cafés where they generally met, most likely the Pelican. Unless, of course, he had gone to a cinema . . .

The broad-shouldered man was not outside. It had

turned cold, and, with the twilight, sheets of blue-gray fog were spreading through the streets, making the lights look faint and woolly. A hoarse voice shouted:

"*Gazette de Liège! . . . Gazette de Liège! . . .*"

René wasn't at the Pelican, nor at any other of their usual haunts. Jean gave up the search. His legs were heavy, and his mind had lost all capacity to think. He decided to go home to bed.

He had scarcely shut the front door behind him when he realized something was wrong. The kitchen door was open. Mademoiselle Pauline, the third roomer, was bending over someone he could not see. Like the others, she was foreign—Polish—and a student.

Jean moved forward in the silence, which was suddenly broken by a sob. Mademoiselle Pauline's homely face took on a severe expression when she saw him.

"Look at your mother, Jean!"

Madame Chabot, in her apron, with her elbows on the kitchen table, was weeping hot tears.

"What's wrong?"

"You ought to know, if anybody does."

Madame Chabot dried her red eyes, looked at her son, and then started off again, worse than before.

"He'll be the death of me. . . . It's too cruel. . . ."

"What have I done, Maman?"

Jean spoke in a strained, toneless, too loud voice. He could feel a curdling terror spreading through his body.

"Thank you, Mademoiselle Pauline," said Madame Chabot. "Leave us alone, if you don't mind. . . . You've been most kind. . . . We've always been poor, but nobody's ever been able to say we weren't respectable."

"What is it, Maman? I don't understand."

The Polish girl left them, though she took care to leave the kitchen door open, and the door of her own room.

"Now, come on! Tell me what you've done. Out with it! Your father will be home in a few minutes. . . . To think it'll be all around the neighborhood!"

"I swear I don't understand."

"You're lying. You've been lying to us ever since you started going with Delfosse and all those filthy women. . . . It was half an hour ago. . . . Madame Velden came rushing here, out of breath. Mademoiselle Pauline was talking to me. And she said—Madame Velden did—that a man had just been into her shop. And it wasn't to buy vegetables! Oh, no! It was to ask a lot of questions about you and your family. There's no doubt about it: he's from the police. . . . Of course he *would* go and ask Madame Velden, of all people! The biggest gossip for half a mile around. Everybody must have heard by this time. . . ."

She was standing now. Mechanically, she poured some boiling water into the coffeepot. Then she took a tablecloth from the drawer.

"So that's the thanks we get for all the sacrifices we've made for you. To have the police on your trail! Who knows, they may even come to the house. . . . I don't know what your father will say, but I know mine would have thrown you out. . . . And to think you're not yet seventeen! You didn't waste much time, did you? . . . But it's your father's fault. Letting you stay out till three and four in the morning. And if I say anything, he always stands up for you."

Jean felt certain Madame Velden's visitor had been the broad-shouldered man. He stared obstinately at the floor.

"So you'll keep it to yourself, will you? You won't tell us what you've done?"

"I've done nothing."

"And it's for doing nothing that the police are after you?"

"How do you know it was a policeman?"

"Who else could it be?"

Anything to put a stop to this painful scene. He plucked up his courage and lied.

"Perhaps it's about a job. The pay's rotten where I am, and I've been looking for something better. Someone might have been sent to make inquiries. It would be only natural."

She looked at him sharply.

"There you go! Lying again!"

"I swear . . ."

"Are you sure you and Delfosse haven't done something? Something worse than hanging around and throwing away money?"

"I swear, Maman . . ."

"In that case, you'd better go yourself and talk to Madame Velden about it. There's no need for her to go spreading a lot of wild rumors."

A key turned in the front door. Monsieur Chabot hung up his coat and came into the kitchen, taking his customary place in the armchair.

"Back already, Jean?"

He was surprised to see his wife's red eyes and the sullen look on the boy's face.

"What's the matter?"

"Nothing . . . I was scolding Jean. I won't have him coming in at all hours. One would think he can't bear to spend an evening at home."

Having finished setting the table, she filled the cups. Monsieur Chabot read his newspaper, and, between mouthfuls, commented on the news.

"Another case that's going to make a lot of noise . . . A corpse in a wicker basket . . . A foreigner, of course, and probably a spy."

Then, changing the subject:

"Has Monsieur Bogdanowsky paid?"

"Not yet. He says he's expecting his money on Wednesday."

"He's been saying that for three weeks. If it doesn't come this time, you'll have to speak seriously to him. . . ."

The air was heavy, full of domestic smells—the coffee, the food, the odor of the room itself—and the air was warmed by the shine of the polished copper saucepans and colored by a garish calendar advertising groceries.

Jean, as he plodded through the meal, was gradually absorbed by this familiar place—until *other* things seemed hardly real at all, until it took quite an effort to believe that a couple of hours earlier he had been in the bedroom of a dancer who was putting on her stockings and showing a great quantity of pale, tired flesh. . . .

"Did you inquire about the apartment building?" asked Monsieur Chabot.

"What building?"

"The one on Rue Féronstrée."

"I . . . I'm afraid I forgot."

"As usual! . . . I hope you're going to bed early tonight. You look as though you could do with some sleep."

"Yes, I am. I'm not going out this evening."

"It'll be the first time this week," put in Madame Chabot, who was not altogether satisfied by her son's assurance. She kept watching his expression.

The mailbox rattled. Certain it was for him, Jean leaped to his feet and rushed to open the front door.

"There's that Delfosse again," said Madame Chabot. "He can't leave Jean alone. If it goes on much longer, I'll have to speak to his parents."

Through the glass-paneled door, she and her husband watched the boys talking in an undertone on the doorstep. More than once Jean looked around, as though afraid of being overheard. Delfosse seemed to be pressing him; Jean to be hanging back.

Suddenly, without returning to the kitchen, he shouted out:

"I'll be back in a minute."

Madame Chabot ran out into the hall to stop him, but she was too late. In feverish haste, Jean had seized his jacket, darted out, and slammed the front door behind him.

"That's how you let him carry on!" she exclaimed as she walked back to the kitchen and resumed her place at the table. "That's the way you've taught him to respect you. If you'd only been stricter from the start . . ."

She dealt with the subject exhaustively as she finished eating. Monsieur Chabot looked longingly at his newspaper, but he didn't dare pick it up until the lecture was over.

"You're sure?"

"Absolutely. I recognized him right away. He used to work in our district."

René looked more hatchet-faced than usual, and as they passed under a streetlight, Jean noticed that his friend was very pale and was puffing his cigarette furiously.

"It's more than I can stand. I've had four hours of it now. Just turn your head and take a look. I can hear his steps."

Jean looked. Less than two hundred yards away a man was strolling in the same direction along Rue de la Loi. Jean couldn't see him clearly at that distance, but the man seemed ordinary enough.

"It began after lunch. Maybe earlier, but I didn't notice him till I sat down outside the Pelican. He chose a table near mine. . . . As soon as I set eyes on him, I knew who he was. He's been a plainclothesman for the last two years. He did a job for us once, when my father called in the police about some stuff that was stolen from the plant.

"Girard's the name, or it might be Gérard—I can't remember exactly. . . . I didn't stay at the Pelican long. Somehow it got on my nerves, his being there so close to me. And then, as I was walking on Rue de la Ca-thédrale, I realized he was following me. I went into another café. He hung around until I came out. I went to the Mondain, and when they put the lights on at intermission, I saw him three rows behind. I can't tell you everything I did after that. I walked all over the place, and jumped in and out of streetcars. And you see! He's still there. . . .

"It's the money I'm worried about. All these notes in my pocket. I'd like to get rid of them. Suppose he searched me—what could I say? . . . If you took them, you could say your boss gave them to you to pay for something or other."

"No!"

René's forehead was beaded with perspiration. There was an anxious but at the same time cruel glint in his eye.

"I *must* do something with them. He's bound to stop us sooner or later. . . . Because, don't forget, we're in this together."

"Have you had supper?"

"I couldn't eat if I tried. Maybe I should throw the money into the Meuse as we cross the bridge."

"Ten to one he'd see you."

"Or I could throw it down the toilet in some café. . . . But wait a minute! Better if you did. Come on! Let's find a café. Any one'll do. . . . And then you can go to the lavatory, while he sits and watches me."

"But suppose he doesn't? Suppose he follows me?"

"He won't. And anyhow you can lock the door, can't you?"

They were still on the quiet residential side of the Meuse, with its empty, badly lighted streets. And all the time the detective's steps rang out behind them. He took no trouble to hide what he was doing.

"Why not the Gai-Moulin? . . . It would seem natural, since we go there almost every night. Besides, it would show we were innocent. If we'd killed the Turk, we'd hardly go back. . . ."

"It's too early."

"We can wait awhile. There's not that much hurry. Girard doesn't seem anxious to catch up with us yet."

They walked on, without speaking another word. After crossing the river, they wandered through the center of town, making sure from time to time that Girard was still following.

Reaching, at last, Rue du Pot d'Or, they saw the bright letters of the name: GAI-MOULIN. It had just opened.

"Let's go in."

Their minds went back to their precipitate flight the night before, and they had to summon all their courage to go in again. Victor was standing at the door with a napkin over one arm, which meant no customers had arrived yet.

"Let's go."

They dragged themselves toward the entrance.

"Good evening, messieurs! . . . You haven't seen Adèle, have you?"

"No. Isn't she here?"

"Not yet. It's strange, because she's always so punctual. . . . Come in. What shall I get you? Port?"

"Yes, port, please."

The place was empty. The four members of the orchestra sat chatting and occasionally glancing at the entrance. Their instruments lay on the floor. Génaro, the proprietor, in his white jacket, was arranging the little English and American flags that adorned the shelves behind the bar.

"Good evening," he called out to Delfosse and Chabot. "How are you this evening?"

"Fine, thanks."

A minute later, the detective appeared. He was a young man, who would have looked quite in place bending over an account book in an office. He sat down near the door.

At a sign from Génaro, the orchestra began playing some jazz. The male professional dancer, who had been writing a letter at the other end of the room, finished his sentence, then went up to the number-two female dancer, and the couple moved lazily around the room.

"Here!"

Keeping his hand below the level of the table, René pushed the bundle of notes at Jean, who hesitated. The detective was watching.

"Now's the time."

At last Jean made up his mind, and his fingers closed on the warm, sticky money. He kept it in his hand: no need to let anyone see him putting something in his pocket. Rising stiffly to his feet, he said, loud enough to be heard:

"I'll be back in a minute."

He was stopped by the proprietor.

"Wait, I'll give you the key. The attendant hasn't turned up yet. I don't know what's the matter with everybody tonight."

The cellar door was open, and through it rose the same damp chill as on the night before, making the boy shiver.

After gulping down his glass of port, René began to feel better. To complete the cure, he helped himself

43

to Jean's glass too. Girard had not budged; so their maneuver had succeeded. Jean had probably already pulled the chain, and the telltale notes were now coursing along, heaven knows where.

Adèle came in, wearing a black satin coat trimmed with white fur. She gave a nod to the musicians and shook Victor's hand in passing.

"Hello!" she said, seeing René. "Isn't your friend here? I saw him this afternoon. He came to my place. A strange boy . . . I'll just go and take my things off."

She left her coat behind the bar, where she exchanged a few words with Génaro. Then she went back and sat down beside René.

"Two glasses? Then you're with somebody?"

"Yes. Jean."

"Where is he?"

"In there."

He jerked his head toward the door at the back.

"Oh, yes . . . What does his father do?"

"He works in an insurance office, I think. Accountant or something."

She didn't ask anything more. It was enough. It was just what she'd thought.

"Why don't you come in your car anymore?"

"It's my father's car. And, as a matter of fact, I haven't got a driver's license. So I only use it when he's away. Next week he's going off to the Vosges. What about a little trip together, you and me? To Spa, for instance?"

"Who's that man? . . . Isn't he a policeman?"

"I . . . I don't know," René stammered, turning red.

"I don't like the look of him. . . . But what's the

44

matter with your friend? Do you think he might have passed out? . . . Victor! A sherry . . . Let's dance. It's not that I want to, but the boss doesn't like the place to look too dead."

Twenty minutes had passed since Jean had disappeared. René danced so badly that finally Adèle took the lead and steered him around the floor. Soon he broke away.

"Excuse me. I must see what's happened to him."

He pushed through the door and looked around. No sign of Jean anywhere. Nobody but the checkroom attendant, who had now arrived and was idly dusting the place.

"Have you seen my friend?"

"No. I've only been here a minute or two."

"You came in by the back way?"

"I always do."

René opened that door. It was raining. The little alley was empty, and the only streetlight was bleakly reflected by the wet cobbles.

—4—

A Night with
the Pipe Smokers

There were four of them sitting in the immense room, which was dismally furnished with tables covered with blotting paper and lamps with green cardboard shades. There were several doors, some of them open, showing rooms beyond.

The four were members of the Sûreté, on night duty. The tall, ginger-haired man sitting on the edge of one of the tables was Inspector Delvigne. From time to time he played with his mustache. A young detective was doodling on the blotting paper in front of him. The one speaking was a short, thickset man who obviously hailed from the country—a peasant from head to foot.

"Seven francs apiece if you order them by the dozen. Pipes you'd pay twenty francs for in any shop . . . Absolutely flawless . . . My brother-in-law works in the factory, at Arlon."

"We might take two dozen, for the whole squad."

"That's what I thought of telling him. . . . By the way, he once gave me an excellent tip for filling pipes. They know a thing or two, those in the trade. . . ."

Delvigne swung his leg from the edge of the table. Everybody listened attentively. Everybody smoked. Blue clouds spread through the diffused light of the lamps.

"You don't stuff the tobacco in any which way. You take the bowl in your hand, like this. . . ."

A door opened, and a man came in, pushing someone in front of him. The inspector looked up.

"Is that you, Perronet?"

"Yes, Chief."

"Just a moment." And to the pipe expert: "Hurry up!"

The young man who had been brought in was left standing near the door, and he had to listen.

"Do you want one too?" the thickset man asked Perronet. "Real brier for seven francs. I can get them through my brother-in-law, who's a foreman at Arlon."

Still swinging his leg, the inspector called out:

"Come over here, young man."

It was Jean Chabot, in the most piteous state imaginable. His eyes were set in such a fixed stare that he looked as though he might go clean out of his mind at any moment. The others, still exchanging views on the subject of pipes, glanced at him as he stepped forward. At some witty remark they all laughed.

"Where did you nab him, Perronet?"

"At the Gai-Moulin. And in the nick of time. He was about to throw a bunch of money down the toilet."

Nobody showed either surprise or interest. The inspector looked at them.

"Who'll fill in the forms?"

The youngest shifted his seat over to where some forms were lying ready.

"Last name, first name, age, profession? . . . Come on! Answer, will you?"

"Chabot . . . Jean-Joseph-Emile . . . Sixteen . . . Clerk."

"Address?"

"Fifty-three Rue de la Loi."

"Previous offenses?"

"None."

The word had a throttled sound.

"Father?"

"Chabot . . . Emile . . . Accountant."

"Has he ever been in trouble?"

"Never."

"Mother?"

"Elizabeth Chabot . . . Forty-two . . ."

"Maiden name?"

"Doyen."

Nobody was listening. These were only the formalities. The inspector with the ginger hair and mustache slowly lit his meerschaum pipe. He stood up, took a few steps, then turned to one of his subordinates:

"I suppose someone's seeing about that suicide on Quai du Coronmeuse?"

"Gerbert's there now."

"Good! . . . Now for you, young man. And if you'd like some good advice, don't beat around the bush. . . . Last night you were at the Gai-Moulin in the

48

company of a certain Delfosse. We'll be dealing with him later. . . . Between you, you didn't have enough money to pay for your drinks. In fact, you hadn't paid for two or three days. . . . Is that right?"

Jean opened his mouth, but he shut it again without uttering a sound.

"Your parents aren't rich, and what you earn won't take you very far. Yet you're out having a rare good time, running up debts all over the place. . . . Well? Is that correct?"

The wretched boy hung his head. He could feel the eyes of the five men on him. Inspector Delvigne spoke condescendingly, even a little contemptuously.

"At the tobacconist's, for instance. Yesterday you owed him money. . . . The old, old story! Boys just out of school, acting like bright young men-about-town, without a penny to do it on. . . . How many times have you stolen money from your father's wallet?"

Jean turned crimson. That last remark was worse than a slap in the face. What made it so dreadful was that he'd earned it; everything the inspector said was true.

Yes, true. More or less. But the truth, put so baldly, was no longer quite the truth.

It had begun by Jean going to the Pelican now and then after work, to have a glass of beer with his friends. That was where they used to meet, and the warm feeling of comradeship was irresistible. Very soon it became a regular thing.

In a moment there, life was transformed; the day's drudgery and the chief clerk's sermons were forgotten. Sitting back in their chairs in the fanciest café the

49

town possessed, they would watch people pass by along Rue du Pont d'Avroy, nod to acquaintances, shake hands with friends, eye the pretty girls, some of whom would occasionally join them at their table. Was not all Liège theirs?

René Delfosse stood more rounds than the others, since he was the only one who had an abundant supply of pocket money.

"What are you doing tonight?"

"Nothing."

"Let's go to the Gai-Moulin. There's a simply terrific dancer there."

That was more wonderful still. Intoxicating. Bright lights, crimson plush, the air filled with music, perfume, and familiarity. Victor had a friendly way of speaking that flattered the boys. But what counted far more were those bare-shouldered women, who would casually lift their skirts to hitch up a stocking.

So the Gai-Moulin had become a habit too. More than a habit—a necessity. One thing, however, marred its perfection. Rarely could Jean take his turn at paying. And once—though only once—to indulge in that luxury, he had helped himself to money that wasn't his. He had taken it, not from his parents, but from the petty cash. Barely twenty francs. It was easily done; he simply charged a little extra on a number of registered letters or other mail he'd taken to the post office.

"I never stole from my father."

"I don't suppose he has very much to steal. . . . But let's get back to last night. You were both at the Gai-Moulin. Neither of you had any money, though

50

that didn't stop you from buying a drink for one of the dancers. . . . Give me your cigarettes."

Unsuspectingly, Jean held out his pack.

"Cork-tipped Luxors? Is that right, Dubois?"

"That's right."

"So! . . . Now, while you were sitting there, a rich-looking man comes in and orders champagne. It wasn't hard to guess that his wallet was well lined, was it? . . . Contrary to your usual habit, you left by the back door, which is near the steps to the cellar. And what should we find this morning on the cellar steps but two cigarette butts and some ash.

"Instead of leaving, you and Delfosse hid. The rich foreigner was killed. Perhaps at the Gai-Moulin, perhaps elsewhere. No wallet was found on him, and no gold cigarette case, though he'd been seen with one that night. . . .

"Today you start paying off your debts. But this evening, knowing you're being followed, you think you'd better throw the rest of the money away. . . ."

This story was told in such a bored voice that it was hard to believe Delvigne took it seriously.

"You see, young man, how easy it is to get in a mess when you once start going wrong! The best thing you can do now is make a clean breast of everything. No doubt that would be taken into account . . ."

The telephone rang. He broke off to answer it, while everyone else listened in silence.

"Hello! . . . Yes . . . Tell her they'll be coming for it any minute now."

Then, to the others:

"It's about the little servant who killed herself. Her

51

mistress wants to be rid of the body as soon as possible."

Jean stared at the dirty floor, his jaws set so tightly, they would have been hard to prize open with a chisel.

"Where did you do the job? . . . At the Gai-Moulin?"

The jaw muscles relaxed.

"It's not true. . . . I'd swear by anything . . . by . . . on my father's head. . . ."

"You can leave your father out of it. It's not going to be much fun for him either."

At these words a shiver ran through the boy. It had been bad enough before, but now he suddenly realized the full horror of his situation. A few more hours, and his parents would know!

"It's not true," he shouted. "I didn't do it. . . . Can't you see . . ."

"Take it easy, young man."

"I tell you, I didn't do it. . . . I didn't do it. . . . I tell you . . ."

In a fury he flung himself at the detective standing between him and the door. He wasn't trying to escape; he wasn't trying to do anything; he was in a frenzy, gasping, gurgling.

The struggle was short, and in a few minutes, still howling, he was on the floor. The others, as they went on smoking, watched the scene, exchanged glances, shrugged.

"A glass of water, Dubois."

One was produced and flung in Jean's face. His outburst subsided into sobbing. Clutching at his throat, he kept saying:

"I tell you . . . I tell you . . ."

With a grimace of disgust, Delvigne growled:

"They're all the same, these little rotters. And soon we'll have his father and mother to entertain!"

It was not unlike a hospital, with a group of doctors gathered around a patient who was putting up a futile struggle against death.

For, kick and scream as he might, what could Jean do? What could he do against five men? Five tough, hard-bitten men . . . Five to one . . .

"Get up!" snapped Delvigne.

Weakly, submissively, Jean stood up. His resistance was broken. All his outburst had accomplished was to leave him utterly washed out. He looked around, like a beast about to be led to slaughter.

"Please!" he whined. "Please . . . I beg you . . ."

"Better tell us where the money came from."

"I don't know. . . . I swear . . . I . . ."

"We've had enough of your swearing."

The boy's black suit was covered with dust. And there were great black smears on his wet face, where he had wiped it with his dirty hands.

"My father's ill. He has a weak heart. . . . Last year he had an attack, and the doctor said if anything upset him, it might . . ."

He spoke in a dull, monotonous voice. A voice without hope.

"It's late in the day to think of that. You should have kept out of trouble. . . . And now, once more, you'd better talk! Who did it? Was it you? Or was it Delfosse? . . . He's another! If he doesn't come to a bad end, it won't be for want of asking. I wouldn't be surprised to find that he was at the bottom of it all."

Another policeman in plain clothes entered the

room. Waving genially to the others, he sat down at
a table and started looking through a file.

"I didn't kill him. I didn't even know . . ."

"All right, my boy. Let's say you didn't kill him."

The inspector's manner had suddenly changed.
His voice was paternal.

"All the same, you know something about it. That
money didn't jump into your hand all by itself. One
day you haven't a franc to your name, and the next
you have so much that you think you'd better throw
it away. . . . Give him a chair, somebody."

It was what Jean needed more than anything.
Hardly able to stand, he was swaying visibly. He sank
down on the cane-seated chair that was shoved under
him and, putting both elbows on the table, sank his
head in his hands.

"There's no hurry. Take your time about it. Just
get it into your head that if anything can save you
now, it's telling everything. No need to despair. You're
not yet seventeen, so you'd go before a juvenile court.
A reformatory's not a prison. Don't forget that."

Suddenly an idea struck the boy, and there was a
gleam of hope in his eyes as, one after the other, he
studied the men around him. Not one of them bore
any resemblance to the broad-shouldered man.

Perhaps he and René had been wrong. Perhaps
the stranger wasn't a policeman at all. In fact, might
he not be the murderer? He'd been at the Gai-Moulin
the night before. And was there when they left. . . .

And if he'd followed them, wasn't that just to
frighten them? So they'd bolt, and thus draw suspicion
on themselves. Jean was almost panting with hope as
he said:

"I think I know who did it. A big man, and strong."

Delvigne shook his head, but Jean was not to be discouraged now.

"He came into the Gai-Moulin almost immediately after the Turk—I mean the Greek. He was alone. . . . And today he followed me, and he asked questions about me at Madame Velden's—that's the greengrocer's near our house."

"What's he talking about now?"

It was Perronet who answered:

"I'm not quite sure. But, as a matter of fact, there was a stranger at the Gai-Moulin last night, a man no one had ever seen there before."

"When did he leave?"

"At the same time as Adèle."

The inspector looked hard at Jean, who was beginning to breathe more freely, but in the conversation that followed he took no further notice of him.

"Tell me exactly—in what order did everybody leave?"

"First of all the two young fellows. At least they pretended to, though it was really to hide in the cellar. Then the musicians, the male dancer and the other woman dancer. Adèle followed a moment or so later, with this man we're talking about."

"That leaves us with the proprietor, Graphopoulos, and the two waiters?"

"No. I forgot. One of the waiters, Joseph, left with the band."

"I see: the proprietor, Graphopoulos, and one waiter. What's his name?"

"Victor. There were only those three—and of course the two in the cellar."

"What happened then?"

"Graphopoulos went next. At least that's what the proprietor says. Then he and Victor switched off the lights and locked the place up."

"And the other man wasn't seen again, the stranger?"

"No. He's described as a big man, with broad shoulders. Speaks with a French accent."

Delvigne refilled his pipe. He looked annoyed.

"Call the Gai-Moulin and ask Girard what's going on."

Jean waited on tenterhooks. It was almost harder to bear now, because of that ray of hope. It was agonizing. Such a bright little ray—yet it might be extinguished at any moment. His hands were clenched on the edge of the table. His eyes darted here and there, always coming back to the telephone.

As one of them asked for the Gai-Moulin, the pipe-maker's brother-in-law returned to the subject of pipes.

"Then it's settled? I'll order two dozen? . . . We'll want straight ones, I suppose."

"Yes, straight for me," answered the inspector, while the others nodded.

"Two dozen straight . . . By the way, do you want me anymore? There's my kid with the measles, and . . ."

"No. You can go."

"Thanks."

The man moved toward the door, then stopped, shot a glance at Jean, and in an undertone asked his chief:

"Keeping him?"

"Don't know yet . . . Anyhow, till tomorrow . . . Then we'll see."

Jean's hands slackened. The ray of hope had gone—gone for good. Tomorrow would be too late. His parents would know.

But he had no tears left. He simply went limp. Vaguely, he heard the voice at the telephone:

"Is that you, Girard? . . . Delfosse still there? . . . What? Dead-drunk? . . . Yes, he's here. He denies everything, of course. . . . Wait. I'll ask the chief."

He turned to Delvigne.

"Girard wants to know what he's to do. The fellow's plastered. He and Adèle have been drinking champagne together, and she's almost as far gone as he is. Girard asks if he should arrest him."

The inspector looked at Jean and heaved a sigh.

"We've got one. That's enough for now. We'll leave Delfosse alone, and maybe he'll give something away. Tell Girard to hang on to him, and call again later."

Inspector Delvigne was sitting in the only arm-chair, with his eyes closed. It might have been thought that he was asleep, except for the thin wisp of smoke that rose from the corner of his mouth.

One of his men was making a fair copy of Jean Chabot's interview. Another was pacing up and down, waiting for it to strike three, when he would be free to go home to bed.

It had indeed turned colder. Even the cloud of smoke seemed cold. Though Jean was still awake, his mind was filled with a dense red-brown fog. His elbows were still on the table and his head in his hands. He shut his eyes, opened them, then shut them again. And each time his eyelids lifted, he found himself staring at the same document, the top of which protruded from a folder. Engrossed in an elegant hand, it dealt with theft:

Procès-verbal, issued to Sieur Joseph Dumourois, day laborer, domiciled at Upper Flémalle, for the theft of rabbits . . .

The rest was hidden.

The telephone rang. The man on his feet stopped pacing and answered it.

"Yes . . . Good . . . Hope he has a good time. No? Too drunk, is he? . . . I'll tell the chief."

He went over to the inspector.

"It was Girard. Delfosse and Adèle left in a taxi, and drove to her place on Rue de la Régence. They went upstairs together. Girard's keeping watch outside."

Through the red-brown fog, Jean had a fleeting vision of the room he'd been in only a few hours before: Adèle's unmade bed . . . Adèle standing over her spirit lamp . . . Adèle dressing . . .

"And that's all you have to tell us? . . . You're quite sure? . . . As I said before, it'll be better for you . . ."

But Jean didn't answer. He couldn't. He simply hadn't the strength. He could hardly take in what was said to him.

A sigh from the inspector, who turned to the man who was waiting for three o'clock.

"All right. You can go. But leave me some tobacco, will you?"

"Do you think you'll get anywhere?" asked the detective, with a jerk of his head toward Jean, whose head and shoulders had now fallen forward, right on the table.

Delvigne merely shrugged.

The fog was gone. There was nothing now in Jean's mind but a huge hole. A huge black pit writhing with strange dark forms. Sometimes a red spark. But the spark gave no light. . . .

He woke with a start when the telephone at last succeeded in drilling its way into his brain. The lamps were still on, but they looked weak and yellow in the dingy daylight that came through three tall windows. The ringing must have waked the inspector too; he was rubbing his eyes. He stood up, aimlessly picked up his pipe, which was lying on the table, and walked stiffly over to the telephone.

"Hello! . . . Yes . . . Yes . . . What's that? . . . No. The boy's here. Been here all night . . . By all means. He can come and see him if it'll do him any good!"

Delvigne moistened his sticky mouth, swallowed a couple of times, and put a match to his pipe as he came over slowly and stood in front of Jean.

"Your father's reported you missing. I think he'll be coming here."

With brutal suddenness the sun thrust its face over the neighboring roofs, turning the gray windows into a blaze of warmth. The cleaners had arrived; there was the sound of pails, splashing and scrubbing.

A confused murmur of voices and vehicles rose from the market, which was only two hundred yards away, opposite the Town Hall. Streetcars passed, ringing stridently, as though it were their special mission to rouse the city to its day's work.

And Jean Chabot sat, with troubled eyes and dirty face, running his fingers through his hair.

— 5 —

Morning

The heavy, harsh breathing stopped. René Delfosse was waking. His eyes opened, and in an instant he was sitting upright, looking around apprehensively.

As at police headquarters, the electric light was still burning, though daylight streamed in through the uncurtained window. In the street below, all was busy as usual.

From beside him came the sound of regular breathing. Adèle, only partly undressed, lay on her stomach, her head buried in the pillow. One shoe was still on, and its high heel dug into the yellow silk eiderdown.

René felt terrible. His tie was almost strangling him. He went to get a drink of mineral water. Unable to find a glass, he drank straight from the bottle. The room was stuffy, and the water tepid. He gulped it down greedily anyway. Then he stared at himself in the mirror over the basin.

His brain worked slowly. He could remember something of the night before, but there were gaps, large completely blank. For instance: how did he happen to be in Adèle's room? He hadn't the least idea. He looked at his watch, only to find it had stopped. Judging by the noise outside, it couldn't be early. And there, across the street, was a bank already open, so it was nine at any rate.

"Adèle!" he called, suddenly finding the silence uncomfortable.

She stirred, turned over on her side, and drew her knees up toward her chin. But didn't wake up.

"Adèle! I have to talk to you. . . ."

He looked at her none too tenderly. Right now she even disgusted him a little. She opened an eye, moved once more, sighed, then fell asleep again.

René's mind was clearing, but that only made him more nervous. His restless eyes were unable to look at anything for longer than a second. He went to the window to see if there was a clock within sight. Instead of a clock, it was Girard he saw, walking up and down on the opposite sidewalk, with his eyes fixed on the door below.

René quickly drew back into the room.

"Adèle! . . . For the love of God, wake up!"

He was scared. He picked his jacket up from the floor. Putting it on, he instinctively felt the pockets. And that focused his mind. Hastily his hands dived into one pocket after another. Not one of them contained so much as a sou.

He drank again, and the tasteless water sat heavily

on his already unhappy stomach. For a moment he thought he'd be sick. So much the better. It would do him good to vomit. But then he found he couldn't.

And the dancer slept on, her hair sprawling over the pillow, her face shiny. An obstinate sleep, as though she were doing it on purpose.

While he was putting his shoes on, he caught sight of her handbag. It gave him an idea. But first he crept to the window to see if Girard was still there. Next he listened to make sure Adèle was breathing regularly.

Cautiously he opened the bag. And there, jumbled up with powder and lipstick and some old letters, were nearly nine hundred francs, which he promptly transferred to his pocket.

She hadn't stirred. He tiptoed to the door, opened it with the utmost care, and quietly went downstairs. He knew there would be a yard in the back. Every grocer's shop must have a yard where they can unload all the barrels and boxes. And equally certainly there would be a way through to the street behind.

He was dying to run, but managed to hold himself down to a reasonable pace. Half an hour later he arrived, bathed in perspiration, at the Gare des Guillemins, where he made straight for the ticket office.

Another detective approached the building on Rue de la Régence.

"What is it?" asked Girard as he shook hands.

"The chief wants you to bring the fellow along, and Adèle too. Here are the warrants."

"Has the other boy confessed?"

"No. He denies everything. He's got some story of

Delfosse stealing the money from a chocolate shop. His father's there. It's not funny, I can tell you."

"Are you coming with me?"

"The chief didn't tell me to. But now that I'm here, I might as well."

They went in together and knocked on Adèle's door on the second floor. There was no answer, so Girard tried the handle. The door opened. As though sensing danger, Adèle was awake at once. Raising herself on one elbow, she asked in a thick voice:

"Who's there?"

"Police. I have a warrant for you. And your friend. Where is he?"

She looked around the room as she got up from the bed. Instinctively her eyes lighted on her handbag. Seeing it open, she pounced on it like a hawk, and feverishly rummaged inside.

"The bastard! He took all my money."

"You didn't know he'd gone?"

"I was fast asleep. . . . But I'll get even with him, the filthy little bastard!"

Meanwhile, Girard's eye had come to rest on a gold cigarette case lying on the bedside table.

"And whose is this?"

"René's, I suppose. I saw him with it last night."

"Get dressed."

"Are you arresting me?"

"The warrant's made out in the name of one Adèle Bosquet, dancer at the Gai-Moulin. I take it that's you?"

"All right!"

She didn't get flustered. As a matter of fact, being

arrested didn't seem to bother her half as much as the theft of her money. As she brushed her hair, she kept muttering:

"The bastard . . . And I was having such a nice sleep."

The two policemen inspected the room like connoisseurs, exchanging an occasional wink.

"Will they be keeping me long? Should I take some extra clothes with me?"

"Haven't the least idea. Our orders are just to deliver you."

She sighed.

"Oh, well! Since I have nothing on my conscience . . ."

Then, moving toward the door:

"I'm ready. . . . I suppose you have a car? . . . No? In that case, I'd just as soon walk by myself. You can follow."

She shut her bag with an angry snap and tucked it under her arm. Girard slipped the gold cigarette case into his pocket.

Outside, she walked briskly to police headquarters, which she entered without a moment's hesitation. It was not until they were in a wide corridor that she finally stopped.

"This way," said Girard. "Wait, though. I'll just ask the inspector whether . . ."

But Adèle had plunged straight into the large room before he could stop her. A quick glance was enough to make her realize that they had been waiting for her; nothing else seemed to be going on. Inspector Delvigne was on his feet. Leaning on an elbow at one of the tables, Jean was trying to swallow a sandwich that had been given to him. Jean's father was standing in a corner staring at the floor.

"And the other one?" asked Delvigne.

"Flown! Must have sneaked out the back way. And according to mademoiselle, he's made off with her money."

Jean was incapable of looking anyone in the face. He put the sandwich down again.

"A nice pair, Inspector! You won't catch me a second time getting mixed up with the likes of them. I can promise you that!"

"Take it easy! All you need do is answer my questions."

"He took all my money, everything I have in the world."

"We've heard enough about that!"

Girard was speaking to the inspector in an undertone. He handed him the gold cigarette case.

"First of all," said Delvigne, "I'd like to know how this object came to be in your room. I suppose you know who it belonged to originally? . . . A certain Graphopoulos, now dead, spent his last evening in your company. And he was seen several times earlier taking this cigarette case from his pocket. Did he make you a present of it?"

She looked at Jean, and then back at the inspector. "No."

"Then how did it get in your room?"

"Delfosse brought it."

Jean looked up sharply and sprang to his feet.

"It's not true. . . . She . . ."

"You, sit down again, and keep your mouth shut.

66

". . . So you tell me that it was René Delfosse who left it with you. You understand, mademoiselle, that you're making a serious accusation?"

"A very serious accusation to make," she sneered, "against a gentleman who's a common thief!"

"Have you known him long?"

"About three months. Ever since he started coming almost every night to the Gai-Moulin with this one here . . . A pretty pair! I ought to have known they were no good. But you know how it is. They're only boys, so I treated them more like pals than customers. I could sit and have a chat with them without feeling it was part of my job. And when they bought me a drink, I was always careful not to ask for anything too expensive. . . . And this is how they pay me back!"

Her expression was hard.

"And you've slept with the two of them, haven't you?"

At that she snorted.

"Not at all! I'm sure that's what they wanted, but they went round and round without daring to make a grab. Both of them have come to my room, with some excuse, to have a look at me dressing."

"The evening of the crime, you were drinking champagne with this Graphopoulos. Was it understood that you were to spend the rest of the night with him?"

"What do you take me for? I'm employed as a dancer."

"As a so-called dancer-hostess, to be precise. We know what that means. You're paid to be nice to them and get them to order drinks. Did you leave together?"

"No."

"Did he suggest anything?"

"I suppose he did. I remember that he gave me the number of his room, but, for the life of me, I couldn't tell you the name of the hotel. I wasn't really listening."

"All the same, you didn't leave alone."

"You're right! As I went out, another customer—sounded like a Frenchman—asked me the way to Place Saint-Lambert. I told him I was going that way myself. But suddenly he said: 'Oh, I've left my tobacco behind.' And he went back."

"A heavily built man?"

"That's the one."

"You went straight home?"

"Same as every other night."

"And you heard about the crime the next day?"

"It was this young fellow who told me. He came to my room in the afternoon."

Two or three times Jean had wanted to intervene, but each time the inspector had quelled him with a look. As for Monsieur Chabot, he was still standing in the same position.

"You have no idea yourself about the murder?"

She didn't answer at once.

"Answer me. Chabot has just been telling us that he and his friend Delfosse were hiding in the cellar. . . ."

Adèle snorted again, more disdainfully than before.

"He says all they were after was the till. But when they came out of their hiding place about a quarter of an hour after the Gai-Moulin had shut, they found the body of Graphopoulos stretched out on the floor."

"Did they really!"

"Apart from them, there are three suspects: Gé-naro, Victor, and that unknown Frenchman. Génaro says Graphopoulos left just after you; then, last of all, he and Victor."

She shrugged, while Jean gave her a look that was both reproachful and supplicating.

"What about Génaro and Victor?" the inspector went on. "Do you think either of them . . . ?"

"That's preposterous," she said contemptuously.

"That leaves the Frenchman, who started off with you, and who went back, either alone or with you."

"And how would he have got in?"

"You've been at the Gai-Moulin long enough to have provided yourself with a duplicate key."

Once more she shrugged. Then, after a pause, she said:

"Even so, it was Delfosse who had the cigarette case. And if he was hiding in the cellar too . . ."

"It's not true, about the cigarette case," shouted Jean. "It was in your room the next day. I saw it in the afternoon. I swear I did."

But Adèle repeated:

"It was Delfosse who . . ."

The rest was lost in the general clamor as everybody began speaking at once, including a policeman who came in just then and said something to the inspector. As the noise subsided, the latter was heard to say:

"Show him in."

The person who appeared was a comfortable, well-fed man of about fifty, whose bulging vest was adorned with a heavy gold watch chain. He had a dignified, even somewhat pompous manner.

"I was requested to call . . ." he began, looking around inquiringly.

"Monsieur Lasnier, I think," said Delvigne. "Will you please take a seat? . . . I'm sorry to bother you, but I would like to know whether there was any money missing from your till yesterday."

The chocolate maker of Rue Léopold opened his eyes wide.

"From the till?"

Monsieur Chabot listened with acute suspense, as though the answer was going to tell him exactly what kind of son he had.

"Suppose, for example, someone had taken two thousand francs from your till. It would have been noticed, wouldn't it?"

"Two thousand francs? . . . I'm afraid I'm rather at a loss . . ."

"If you'd just answer the question . . . Do you know if any money was missing yesterday?"

"Not a sou."

"Your nephew visited you, didn't he?"

"Wait a moment . . . Yes, I think he did look in. He often does—not so much to see me as to get a supply of chocolates."

"You've never noticed that he had taken money from your till?"

"Monsieur!"

The man was indignant. He seemed to call them all to witness the enormity of the suggestion.

"My brother-in-law is wealthy enough," he went on stiffly, "to provide his son with all he needs."

"I beg your pardon, Monsieur Lasnier. I was obliged to ask the question. Thank you."

"Is that all you have to . . . ?"

"It's all I have to ask you. Yes."

"But whatever made you think . . . ?"

"I'm afraid I can say nothing further for the present. Girard, will you show Monsieur Lasnier out."

As the inspector started pacing up and down, Adèle asked:

"Do you need me any longer?"

She didn't insist, however; the look Delvigne gave her was eloquent enough.

And then for nearly ten minutes not a single word was spoken. They seemed to be waiting for something or somebody. Monsieur Chabot was longing to smoke, but he didn't dare ask if he might. Nor had he the courage to look at his son. All he did, therefore, was stand still and keep quiet, and he looked the picture of embarrassment, like an indigent patient in a fashionable doctor's waiting room.

As for Jean, his eyes were glued to Delvigne, and every time the inspector passed, he seemed on the point of speaking to him.

At last steps were heard in the corridor, and there was a knock on the door.

"Come in."

Two men entered: Génaro, proprietor of the Gai-Moulin, short and thickset, wearing a gray sports jacket; and Victor. Jean had never seen the latter in anything but his waiter's apron and white shirt.

Dressed all in black, he looked strangely ecclesiastical.

"I got your message an hour ago," began the Italian excitably, "but I couldn't very well . . ."

The inspector cut short his explanations.

"Yes, yes. We won't go into that. What I want to know is whether you saw this cigarette case last night in the hands of René Delfosse."

Génaro made a slight deprecating bow.

"For my part, I don't have much to do with the customers. Perhaps Victor can tell you."

"Very well. You answer."

Jean, breathing hard, looked searchingly at the waiter. But Victor looked down with lowered eyelids and in an almost demure voice said:

"I wouldn't like to say anything that might harm the two young gentlemen. They've always treated me very well. But I suppose I must tell the truth."

"Come on! Answer yes or no."

"Well . . . Yes, he had it. In fact, I even hinted to him he'd better be careful."

"That's a lie if ever there was one," Jean burst out. "Victor! Haven't you any sense of decency? . . . Listen, Inspector . . ."

"Shut up! . . . Now tell me what you know about the financial situation of these two young men."

Victor seemed embarrassed by the question. Reluctantly, he said:

"They certainly have been getting into debt. And not only for their drinks. I've had to lend them small amounts of money from time to time."

"You noticed Graphopoulos, of course. What sort of a man did you take him for?"

"A rich foreigner, traveling. They're our best cus-

72

tomers. You could tell he was rich by the way he ordered champagne, without asking the price. Besides, he gave me a fifty-franc tip."

"Did you see what he had in his wallet? Any thousand-franc notes?"

"A lot of them. But they were French ones. I only saw hundred-franc notes in Belgian money."

"That's all you noticed?"

"Yes. Except that he was well dressed and had a big pearl tiepin."

"When did he leave?"

"A little after Adèle, who left with the other customer. A hulking great brute, who drank only beer and gave me one franc for a tip. He was smoking French tobacco."

"That left only you and the proprietor. Did you stay long?"

"No longer than it took to put our things on, switch off the lights, and lock up."

"You went straight home?"

"As usual. Monsieur Génaro left me at the end of the street where he lives—Rue Haute-Sauvenière."

"When you got to work next morning, did you notice anything unusual? Any blood?"

"Not a sign of anything. I was there when our cleaners went over the place."

Génaro was listening with an absent air, as though the interview did not concern him. But now the inspector turned to him.

"Is it true that you generally leave the night's proceeds in the till?"

"Who told you that?"

"Never mind who. Answer my question."

"I always take the money with me. All, that is, but small change."

"What do you mean by small change?"

"Perhaps fifty francs. Never much more."

"That's not true!" Jean fairly screamed. "Dozens of times I've seen him leave . . ."

Génaro cut him short:

"What! So he's the one who told you that lie!"

He looked genuinely astonished. Turning toward the dancer, he added:

"Adèle can tell you . . ."

"Certainly I can."

"What I can't understand is how this young man can say that they saw the body lying in the Gai-Moulin. Graphopoulos left before I did. There's no room for a mistake on that point. And he couldn't have got in again—not unless he broke in, and there was no sign of that."

"So you're telling me . . ."

"The crime had to be committed somewhere else. And I have no idea where. . . . I'm sorry to have to contradict their story so emphatically. They weren't very grand customers, but I couldn't help having a soft spot for them. The proof of that is that I gave them credit, though ordinarily I never dream of doing such a thing. . . . But there it is: the truth's the truth. And this is too serious a case for . . ."

"Thank you."

There was a pause. Then Génaro asked:

"Are there any other questions I can answer?"

"No. You can go, and the waiter too. If I want you again, I'll send for you."

"You've no objection to my keeping the place open?"

"None whatever."

Adèle thought it was a good moment to try again.

"What about me?"

"Run along."

"You're releasing me?"

The inspector didn't answer. He looked thoughtful, even worried, as he stood fingering the bowl of his pipe.

When the three witnesses had gone, the room suddenly seemed very empty. The other policemen had disappeared one after the other, and there was now no one left but Inspector Delvigne, Jean Chabot, and Jean's father. There was a long, oppressive silence.

It was Monsieur Chabot who broke it, though only after long and painful hesitation. First he coughed; then he murmured:

"Excuse me . . . but do you really think . . . ?"

"Do I really think what?" asked the inspector gruffly.

"I don't know. . . . But it seems to me . . ."

He wound up the sentence with a gesture, a vague gesture, which meant:

It seems to me that there's something not quite right in all this.

Jean stood up. The flat contradiction of his story had given him a certain courage. Enough, anyhow, to make it possible for him to look his father in the face.

"They're lying," he said in a clear voice. "They're lying, all of them. I swear they are." Then, turning to Delvigne:

"Don't you believe me?"

No answer.

"And you, Father? Do *you* believe me?"

Monsieur Chabot looked away and finally stammered:

"I . . . I don't really know. . . ."

Then he hastily added:

"The thing to do is find that Frenchman."

Evidently the inspector was finding it hard to make up his mind. He paced furiously, as though trying to walk off his doubts.

"Well, Delfosse has bolted," he muttered, more to himself than to the Chabots.

He continued walking, and it was quite a while before he added:

"Two people swear to his having the cigarette case."

Still on the march, his train of thought could be followed in his mutterings:

"And the two youngsters hiding in the cellar . . . Then last night one of them tries to get rid of a bundle of notes. . . . And . . ."

He stopped dead, and looked in turn at the Chabots.

"And Lasnier won't admit that anything was stolen from his shop."

He walked out of the room, leaving father and son alone together. They took no advantage of the privacy, however, and when he returned, he found them standing where he'd left them, each withdrawn into obstinate silence.

"I couldn't do anything else. . . . I've telephoned the examining magistrate, and from now on the case is in his hands. He won't hear of bail. If you have any favor to ask, you must ask him. It's Monsieur de Conninck."

"François de Conninck?"

"I think that's his Christian name."

With head lowered and shame on his face, Monsieur Chabot murmured:

"We were at school together."

"Well, go and see him if you think it will do any good. But I doubt that it will. I know him. Meantime, I have orders to take the boy to Saint-Léonard."

The words alone were a catastrophe. Doom had been pronounced. Before that, nothing irretrievable had happened. But now . . .

Saint-Léonard Prison: the ugly black building that stood opposite Pont-Maguin, disfiguring a whole district of Liège; a building with medieval turrets, narrow loopholes, and iron bars. . . .

Jean said nothing. He had turned deadly pale.

"Girard!" the inspector called, opening the door. "Order a car and take two men . . ."

The words were enough.

They waited.

"Of course there would be no harm in your going to see Monsieur de Conninck," the inspector said slowly, for the sake of saying something. "If you were at school together . . ."

But his face betrayed what he was thinking. He was measuring the distance that separated the magistrate, son of a line of magistrates, related to all the most influential families of the town, and the accountant for an insurance company, whose son admitted that he had wanted to steal from the till of a nightclub.

"All ready, Chief," said Girard, appearing in the doorway. "Ought I to . . . ?"

Something glittered in his hands. The inspector shrugged, but his eyes said yes.

It was a rite that was carried out so often that it took only a couple of seconds. Girard seized Jean's two hands. There was a steely snap. The boy's father did not realize what was happening until it was over.

Handcuffs! And there would be two uniformed men outside, standing by a car.

"Come along."

Jean took a few steps forward. It seemed as if he would go without a word. At the door, however, he turned. His voice was hardly recognizable.

"On my word of honor, Father . . ."

He was interrupted by a new arrival.

"Well, now, about those pipes, Chief. I thought we might order three dozen after all."

The brother-in-law of the pipemaker foreman was suddenly brought to a standstill by the sight of young Chabot and the glint of steel at his wrists.

"Ah! So you've . . ."

The gesture he made signified: "Got him!"

Delvigne pointed to Monsieur Chabot, who had sat down at one of the tables. With his head in his hands, he was sobbing like a woman.

It was in a discreetly hushed voice that the newcomer went on:

"If we have any left over, we'll have no trouble selling them to the other divisions. At that price . . ."

A car door slammed. The whirr of a starter, the grind of gears.

The inspector was uncomfortable.

"You know," he said, turning to Monsieur Chabot, "the boy's only under arrest."

It was pity, not truthfulness, that made him add:

"Particularly if Monsieur de Conninck's a friend of yours. That'll make things easier. . . ."

Jean's father, beating a lame retreat, managed to summon a sickly smile of gratitude.

—6—

The New Suspect

At one o'clock the afternoon dailies appeared on the streets. Glaring headlines on the wicker-basket murder were on every front page. The Catholic paper, the *Gazette de Liège*, bluntly announced the guilt of Chabot and Delfosse, saying:

CRIME COMMITTED BY TWO YOUNG SINNERS

The headline in the *Wallonie Socialiste* was:

CRIME COMMITTED BY TWO YOUNG BOURGEOIS

Jean Chabot's arrest was reported, and the flight of René Delfosse. The houses of the two boys had been photographed, and comment extended to their parents.

Immediately after the pathetic interview at the Sûreté with his son, Monsieur Chabot shut

80

himself in his house and has since refused to see anyone. Madame Chabot is so affected by the shock that she had to take to her bed. . . .

I was able to catch Monsieur Delfosse just as he returned from Huy, where his bicycle factory is situated. An energetic man, some fifty years of age, with a clear and unflinching eye. Far from being unnerved by the news, he is emphatic about his son's innocence, and intends to lose no time in taking up the cudgels on his behalf. . . .

At Saint-Léonard Prison it is reported that Jean Chabot is perfectly calm. He is awaiting the visit of his lawyer, in whose company he will appear this afternoon before Monsieur de Conninck, the examining magistrate, who is taking charge of all further investigations.

Rue de la Loi wore its usual humdrum aspect. Children could be seen in twos and threes entering the schoolyard, where, yelling and romping, they made use of every minute before they were called inside.

Between the cobblestones of the street grew tufts of grass. The housewife of Number 48 was vigorously scrubbing her doorstep. When the schoolyard emptied, her scrubbing was the only sound left to disturb the afternoon quiet, except for occasional hammer blows on the anvil at a coppersmith's nearby.

Yet, more often than usual, a front door would open. A head would emerge, and a curious glance would be cast at Number 53. And if the inquisitive viewer found her neighbor in the same position, she would not miss the opportunity for a moment's gossip.

"Really! Do you think he could have done it? . . . Why, he's only a boy. . . . To think, not so long ago he was playing here on the sidewalk with my youngsters! . . ."

"Not yet seventeen! But, there you are! When they once start drinking . . . Many's the time I've seen him coming home the worse for liquor. Only the other day I was saying to my husband . . ."

And every quarter of an hour the doorbell rang at Number 53. It was Mademoiselle Pauline who answered it.

"Monsieur and Madame Chabot are not in," she would say with her strong Polish accent.

"*Gazette de Liège*. Would you kindly tell them that . . . ?"

And the reporter would crane his neck to get a glimpse inside. If he was lucky, he might just catch sight of the rounded back of a man sitting in the kitchen.

"It's no use. They're not here."

"But . . ."

She shut the door in their faces, and they had to be content with what they could glean from the neighbors.

One paper, however, struck a different note by asking:

WHERE IS THE BROAD-SHOULDERED MAN?

Under this headline it said:

So far, everybody has been inclined to take the guilt of Delfosse and Chabot for granted.

82

Without wishing to condone their conduct, and confining ourselves to an impartial scrutiny of the facts that have so far come to light, we feel that sufficient attention has not been paid to the disappearance of an important witness—the broad-shouldered stranger who was in the Gai-Moulin on the night of the crime.

According to the waiter who served him, this person was a Frenchman, who had never visited the place before. Nor did he return there last night. Has he already left the city? Has he good reason for not coming forward?

These questions merit investigation. If the two boys should turn out to be innocent, the broad-shouldered man might well be the person to step into their shoes.

As a matter of fact, we have reason to think that Inspector Delvigne, who is acting in close cooperation with the examining magistrate, has not overlooked this aspect of the case. It is rumored that orders have been circulated with a view to ascertaining the stranger's identity and present whereabouts.

This newspaper appeared a little before two o'clock. At three, a florid, corpulent man arrived at police headquarters and asked to see Inspector Delvigne.

"I'm the manager of the Hotel Moderne on Rue du Pont d'Avroy."

"Well?"

"I returned from Brussels a couple of hours ago;

83

and I've just heard about what's been happening here. I think I can give you some useful information."

"About the Frenchman?"

"Yes. And about the victim too."

"Good. Sit down and tell us."

"It was on Wednesday night that the crime was committed, wasn't it?"

"Yes."

"Well, it was on Wednesday, toward the end of the afternoon, that a visitor arrived, a dark man with a strong foreign accent. His only luggage was a pigskin suitcase. I took him upstairs myself. I think the hall porter was on the phone at the time—at any rate, he says he never really saw the man. He took a large front room on the second floor, Number 18, and I left him there.

"I'd hardly reached the hall when another man came in. A broad-shouldered man with a French accent. He asked to see the best rooms. I took him up, and he looked in all the front rooms on the second floor."

"Not Number 18?"

"No. He wanted to. But I told him it had just been taken, and that the gentleman was there. Finally he chose Number 17. . . . I didn't ask either of them to fill out a form. As a rule, the hall porter sees to that; catches them at a convenient moment, generally as they're going in or out."

"You know very well that a registration form has to be filled in on arrival."

"Yes . . . Of course . . . But the hall porter was still at the telephone when they came down, one after the other, and went out. He says he never really saw Number 18 at all. As for Number 17 . . .”

The manager hurried on breathlessly, anxious not to dwell on this part of the story. The police were nasty sometimes when a registration form was not filled in.

“Number 17 stayed till this morning, but the hall porter says he was busy every time the man passed yesterday. And it was only this morning, when he came down and paid his bill, that the hall porter had a chance to ask him about it. ‘I don’t think you filled in a form,’ he said. But the man merely grunted something about its not being worthwhile, and walked straight out. And because the telephone was ringing . . .”

“It’s this one, Number 17, you take to be the broad-shouldered Frenchman?”

“Yes. He left about nine. He had only a light bag, so he didn’t ask for a taxi.”

“And the other one?”

“Number 18? Nothing was seen of him since he came down soon after I’d shown him to his room. He never rang for breakfast, and the room was locked all yesterday and this morning.”

“Was the key on the board?”

“It was there Wednesday evening, but not since then. Apparently he’d come back and then gone out again, taking it with him. As soon as they told me about it, I thought I’d better investigate. I have a skeleton key, of course.”

“What did you find?”

“Nothing but the pigskin suitcase. It had never been unpacked, and the bed had not been slept in.

On the suitcase were the initials E. G. Then the hall porter guessed, and he told me about what he'd read in the papers. Number 18 was obviously the man found dead in the basket, at the Zoo."

"On Wednesday afternoon, you say? . . . And one followed close after the other, as if they'd come by the same train?"

"Yes. The Paris express."

"And they left the hotel soon after?"

"One on the heels of the other. Number 18 was never seen again. Whereas the Frenchman left this morning . . . I'm very sorry about the forms. . . . And I'd be extremely grateful if the name of the hotel could be kept out of the papers. People are so nervous, and it could do a lot of harm."

His request was in vain, however, because at that very moment one of the waiters of the Hotel Moderne was telling exactly the same story to a reporter. At five o'clock, in the final editions, there was a fresh spate of headlines:

NEW LIGHT ON MYSTERY

PLOT THICKENS

BROAD-SHOULDERED FRENCHMAN THE MURDERER?

It was a lovely day. A stream of humanity flowed through the sunny streets, unaware of the eyes scrutinizing them. Every policeman on duty was looking for a weedy youth and a placid, broad-shouldered man. At the stations, however, people could hardly fail to notice that they were being examined from head to foot.

On Rue du Pot d'Or, a truck was drawn up in front

of the Gai-Moulin. Cases of champagne were hauled out and carried into the cool darkness. Génaro, in his shirtsleeves, a cigarette between his lips, checked the cases as they passed. His lips curled slightly in a contemptuous smile each time a passerby whispered excitedly to his companion:

"That's the place!"

Their steps would slow for a moment or two as they tried to peer through the doorway. They had to be content with the glimpse of a crimson plush seat and a marble-topped table.

At nine the lights were switched on, and the orchestra started tuning up. By quarter past nine, half a dozen reporters were at the bar, plunged in eager discussion.

At half past, the place was more than half full, a thing that didn't happen more than once a year, if that. Most of the customers were the young crowd that usually frequented the nightclubs of Liège, but there were others of a different stamp altogether—people who had never in their lives set foot in any such den of debauchery. But curiosity had been aroused. Serious and frivolous alike, all wanted to have a look.

Just to have a look. Nobody had come for anything but that. Nobody danced except the man and woman who were paid to. Dozens of eyes were focused in turn on Génaro, Victor, and the band members. After a drink or two it wasn't difficult to find a pretext for going to have a look at the famous cellar stairs.

"Come on, there! Look sharp!" snapped Génaro

to the two waiters, who were being rushed off their feet. The next minute he was making signs to the musicians to put more life into it. Leaning over toward a woman, he said in an undertone:

"You haven't seen Adèle, have you? She should have been here long ago."

It was important. Adèle, of course, was the chief attraction. People had come to see her, more than anything else.

"Look!" said one of the reporters to a fellow member of the press. "They're here too."

He nodded toward two men who were sitting at a table near the plush curtain that hung across the entrance. Inspector Delvigne was drinking beer, the foam of which was visible on his ginger mustache. By his side Girard was studying the customers face by face.

By ten o'clock, the evening was in full swing, and the Gai-Moulin was almost unrecognizable. Instead of its meager handful of more or less regular customers, with an occasional bird of passage on the lookout for a companion with whom to while away the evening, the place was packed with citizens of both sexes and all ages, and no fewer than twenty cars were parked outside. Most uncommon was the presence of the press. One editor was there in person.

The two detectives watched quietly, taking no part in the animation around them. People were hailing each other from table to table. There were nods and handshakes in all directions. And, of course, all were united by a common topic of conversation.

"Is anything going to happen?"

"Don't shout! That fellow over there is Inspector

Delvigne. You don't imagine he'd come all this way for nothing, do you?"

"Which is Adèle?"

"She doesn't seem to be coming."

But she *did* come, sauntering in in grand style, wearing a loose black satin coat lined with white silk, and making quite a stir. She strolled casually over to the band and shook hands with the leader.

Flashbulb. One of the newspaper photographers had taken a shot for his paper. Adèle merely lifted her shoulders, as though this sudden popularity had no effect on her.

"Five glasses of port, five!"

Victor and Joseph were darting back and forth, threading their way between the tables.

It was almost like a party. A strange party, though, one where everybody had come, not to take part, but to look on. The professional dancers pursued their solitary occupation.

"Really, I can't see that it's anything very remarkable," said a woman to her husband, who had never before taken her to such a place. "It seems quite respectable to me."

Génaro went up to the two policemen.

"Excuse me, Inspector, but shall we do things as usual? Ordinarily, Adèle would dance now."

Delvigne shrugged, without even looking at Génaro.

"I thought I'd better ask," the proprietor went on. "I don't want to upset your plans in any way."

Adèle was at the bar, surrounded by the reporters, who were bombarding her with questions.

"Did Delfosse really make off with your money? How long have you been together?"

"We've never been together!"

"You were drinking champagne with Graphopoulos. What did you think of him?"

"He was all right, in his way . . . But that's enough questions. Leave me alone."

She wandered off to get rid of her coat. Then she went up to Génaro to ask:

"Am I to dance?"

He couldn't make up his mind. He looked at the horde of customers with anxiety, as if he was afraid of being submerged.

"I'd like to know what they're expecting."

A stout matron said loudly:

"It's preposterous, paying ten francs for a glass of lemonade. And there's nothing to see."

She was wrong. There *was* something to see, though only for those who knew the new arrival. Because she had hardly spoken when the plush curtain was drawn aside to admit a middle-aged, silver-mustached man.

He hesitated, taken aback by the sight of such a crowd. In fact, he would have withdrawn discreetly if his eye had not caught that of one of the reporters, who promptly nudged his neighbor. Now that the man had been recognized, there was nothing for it but to go through with the business he had come for.

He was obviously a man who paid a lot of attention to his appearance. Indeed, he was dressed with an elegance not seen every day. As he finally moved forward, carelessly flicking the ash off his cigarette, you could tell he was someone who knew his way in the world, night life included.

He walked up to the bar, making straight for Génaro.

"You are the proprietor?"

"Yes, monsieur."

"Monsieur Delfosse. I understand my son owes you some money."

"Victor!"

Victor hurried toward them.

"Monsieur René's father. He wishes to know how much his son owes."

"Just a minute. I've got it all written down. . . . Here we are! A hundred and fifty francs . . . seventy-five . . . ten . . . and a hundred and twenty yesterday. . . . Is it for Monsieur René alone, or for his friend too?"

Monsieur Delfosse simply handed him a thousand-franc note and said coldly:

"Keep the change."

"Thank you, monsieur! Thank you very much. Won't you have something while you're here?"

But Monsieur Delfosse had turned his back and was moving toward the door without looking at anybody. He passed close to the inspector, but he didn't know him. At the curtain he brushed past another new arrival; without taking the smallest notice, he walked out and got in his car.

Yet it was this second man who was to be the principal event of the evening. He was large and broad-shouldered, with heavy features and a mild expression.

Adèle noticed him first, because she was almost continuously looking toward the door. Her eyes opened wide as he walked straight up to her and held out a fleshy hand.

"Hello again. How are you?"

She made an effort to smile.

"All right, thanks. And you?"

The reporters were already whispering:

"Pray God it's him. What more could we ask for?"

"No! You don't really think he'd be such a fool. . . ."

As if out of bravado, the man pulled from his pocket a little gray package of French tobacco and started filling his pipe.

"A pale ale!" he called to Victor, who, holding a tray above his head, was passing by.

Victor nodded. As he passed the two detectives, he quickly whispered:

"That's him."

How did the news spread? A minute later there was hardly an eye in the place that was not riveted on the broad-shouldered man, who was half-sitting on a stool at the bar, one foot on the floor, the other dangling, and sipping his English beer while contemplating the crowd through the misty glass.

Génaro was obliged to snap his fingers three times before the musicians collected their wits and started to play again. The male professional dancer selfishly maneuvered his partner so as to keep the view for himself. If anyone looked away from the Frenchman, it was only to glance at the two policemen and try to interpret the signs they were exchanging.

At last Delvigne nodded, and the two of them stood

up. With slow, casual movements they sauntered up to the Frenchman. Facing him, Delvigne rested one elbow on the bar; Girard stood ready to seize him from behind.

The music didn't stop. Yet everybody had the same impression: that of an unnatural silence.

Delvigne spoke:

"Excuse me. I believe you've been staying at the Hotel Moderne."

A ponderous look before the answer:

"What of it?"

"I believe you forgot to fill in your registration form."

Adèle, about nine feet away, stared at the Frenchman as though fascinated. There was a loud pop, as Génaro uncorked a bottle of champagne.

"If you have no objection, I'd like you to come and fill it in at my office. And let's have no trouble."

Examining the man's features, Delvigne wondered what there was about him that was so impressive.

"Come along."

"Just a moment."

The man put his hand in his pocket, and Girard, thinking it was for a gun, hastily drew his own.

The bystanders sprang to their feet. A woman screamed. But it was only a few coins that the broad-shouldered man produced from his pocket. Throwing them on the counter, he said:

"Lead the way."

Their exit was far from discreet. If they hadn't been frightened by the sight of Girard's gun, people would no doubt have lined up on either side. Delvigne went first, then the Frenchman, then Girard, who felt he'd made a fool of himself and was red in the face.

The photographer wanted to take a picture, but he couldn't get to the door in time and had to content himself with a back view.

A car was waiting by the curb.

"Get in, will you?"

It was no more than three minutes' drive to the Sûreté. The men on night duty were playing piquet and drinking mugs of beer, sent in from the café around the corner.

The Frenchman entered as though he felt quite at home. He lighted his big pipe, which suited his heavy jowls.

"Let's see your papers."

Delvigne was unaccountably nervous. Though he didn't know why, there was something he didn't like about the way things were going.

"Don't have any."

"Where's your luggage?"

"I have no idea!"

A hard look from Delvigne, whose face then clouded. Really, it was as if this Frenchman were thoroughly enjoying himself.

"Name, address, profession . . . ?"

"Is that your private office?"

An open door showed a small, dark room.

"What's that got to do with you?"

"Come!"

It was the broad-shouldered man who led the way, switched on the light, and shut the door behind them.

"Inspector Maigret. Police Judiciaire, Paris," he said, puffing merrily at his pipe. "Well, my dear colleague, I think we've done a good night's work. . . . And I must say, that's a mighty fine pipe you have."

—7—

Delvigne Embarrassed

"Perhaps you'd better lock the door. We don't want anyone bursting in. Above all, no reporters."

Delvigne turned the key.

"Thanks. Now we can talk things over in peace."

The Belgian looked at his French colleague with that involuntary deference that is paid in the provinces—and especially in Belgium—to all who hail from Paris. Moreover, Delvigne was embarrassed by the mistake he had made. He began to murmur an apology, but Maigret brushed it aside.

"Nothing of the kind! I'd set my heart on being arrested. What's more, you're going to have me clapped in jail, where I'll cool my heels as long as is necessary. . . . And I suggest that you let as few of your men as possible into the secret."

Maigret spluttered as he tried not to laugh out loud, lest they hear in the next room. But the sight of Delvigne's face made it difficult. The inspector was looking uneasily at Maigret, wondering what attitude to adopt. Afraid of making a fool of himself, he couldn't decide whether to take Maigret seriously or to treat the whole thing as a joke.

He was put at ease, however, by Maigret's stifled guffaw, and his features relaxed into a quiet laugh.

"So you want me to lock you up. That's a good one!"

"I tell you it's absolutely necessary."

"Surely not!"

But then Delvigne, more bewildered than ever, saw that his companion was in earnest. They were sitting now, facing each other across a table covered with files. Now and then Maigret glanced at Delvigne's meerschaum pipe with admiration.

"I'd better tell you the whole story. . . . I must apologize for having kept you in the dark. But it seemed to me that it might be better to play a lone hand. I feel sure you'll agree with me. . . .

"The crime was committed on Wednesday, wasn't it?"

"That's right."

"Well, on Monday I was sitting in my office on the Quai des Orfèvres. I was brought a business card: Ephraim Graphopoulos. Before seeing him I called the Aliens Section, as usual, to find out who he was. They could tell me nothing except that he was not a resident of Paris.

"When he came in, he struck me as a man who had something heavy on his mind. He told me he traveled a great deal, and he had reason to think his life was in danger. He wanted to know whether it was possible, and what it would cost, to be followed by a detective day and night.

"Nothing unusual about that. When I told him the cost, he insisted that really good men be put on the job. On the other hand, he answered evasively when I asked him who his enemies were, and just what he was afraid of.

"He gave his address as the Grand Hotel, and that evening I had a man stationed there.

"He seemed to be rich, and on Tuesday morning it occurred to me that the Greek Embassy might be able to tell me something about him. They said he was the son of one of the biggest bankers in Athens, and that he spent his life traveling all over Europe, throwing his money around and having a good time."

"I guess you decided he was simply a playboy."

"We did. . . . But wait!

"On Tuesday evening, the man who had been following him that day came in to report. He couldn't make his man out at all. Graphopoulos had spent most of the day trying to shake him. All the usual tricks: in by one door, out by another; taking taxi after taxi; jumping in and out of buses. But he hadn't succeeded.

"Our man had kept on his heels, and had seen him buy a ticket for London, reserving a seat in the plane leaving Wednesday morning.

"The fellow intrigued me, and I must say I was tempted by the idea of flying to London. So, first thing Wednesday morning, I took over the job.

"Graphopoulos left his hotel at the time I expected. But I was done out of my plane trip. Instead of going to Le Bourget, he taxied straight to the Gare du Nord, where he bought a ticket for Berlin.

"We traveled together, in the same railway car. I really can't say whether he recognized me or not. But he barely looked at me, and we never exchanged a word. When he left the train at Liège, I did the same. He took a room at the Hotel Moderne, and I took one next door. We both had dinner in a restaurant behind the Royal Theater."

"I know it," Delvigne interrupted. "The Bécasse. You get a pretty good meal there, don't you?"

"Particularly the kidneys à la liégeoise. I've never had any better. . . .

"But if he took me to the best restaurant, that's not to say he knew Liège. Graphopoulos gave me the definite impression that he was a stranger here. If he found his way around, it was only by asking. At the station they sent him to the Moderne, and at the hotel they told him about the Bécasse. And there a waiter spoke of the Gai-Moulin."

"So it was only by chance that you ended up there?" asked Delvigne thoughtfully.

"Unless there was a special reason for his choosing the Gai-Moulin. The waiter had mentioned several places.

"I entered the nightclub a few minutes after him. He was sitting at a table with one of the dancers. Nothing surprising in that. I can't say I enjoyed myself; places like that bore me to tears.

"I expected her to go home with him. When I saw her leaving alone, however, I walked with her a short way. Long enough to ask her two or three questions. She told me she'd never seen Graphopoulos before; that he'd asked her to his room, but she was not going; and that he was a crashing bore.

"Having learned that much, I retraced my steps, only to find the Gai-Moulin shut for the night."

"No lights inside?"

"Not a glimmer. I went back to the hotel, but when I saw the key to Number 18 hanging on the board in the hall, I knew I'd lost the track of my man. It didn't worry me much, but I thought I'd better at least have a look. A policeman gave me the names of four or five nightclubs I'd find still open. I checked them conscientiously. But no trace of the Greek."

"A queer business," Delvigne said as Maigret paused.

"The state of the two boys at the Gai-Moulin had not been lost on me. They were as nervous as could be, and I couldn't help wondering whether they had any connection with my mission. Not that they looked at all like the sort who might be threatening the Greek's life. On Thursday, I wandered around the cafés, and ran into them at the Pelican. They were in a far worse state than on the previous evening. Since I'd lost sight of Graphopoulos, I thought it would do no harm to keep an eye on them."

"Did they know you were following them?"

"Oh, yes. I made no bones about it. And it seemed to scare them out of their wits, which only made them all the more interesting.

"Then the papers appeared, announcing the murder. . . . I was of two minds about what to do. I thought of coming straight to you. But finally, as I said before, I thought I could be more useful if I kept under cover. . . . After all, I know what official investigations are like! You have to haul everybody in and question them. . . ."

Maigret eyed Delvigne to see how he was taking all this. Fairly well, it seemed.

"And of course everybody's put on guard . . . and it's always hard to keep things out of the papers . . . No. It seemed to me that for the moment the less you knew about it, the better. . . .

"But it didn't take you long to get on the track of the two boys yourself. When you arrested Chabot, you cut the ground from under my feet. . . .

"But when I heard I was a suspect, that gave me another part to play. I jumped at it. . . . And here I am."

"What's the game?"

"First, tell me this: Do you really think those boys are guilty?"

"To be quite frank . . ."

"Exactly. You don't think so for a moment. And the murderer is hardly likely to think you will. He must feel sure you're following other clues, and he'll be watching his step with the utmost care. But if the broad-shouldered man, as he's called, is arrested, that will put quite a different face on the matter. You'll be able to make a very good case against me. The fact that I arrived here by the same train as Graphopoulos and took a room next door to his is pretty good for a start."

"It's a point, certainly. But I don't know . . ."

"You'll have plenty against me. You'll see! . . . When the public hears of my arrest, it'll be only too pleased. A boy like this Chabot doesn't really fit the part at all. . . . And it will fool the real murderer too. At least there's a good chance of it, and thus a good chance of putting him off guard. . . . Saint-Léonard, isn't it? I think that's the name of your prison."

"You really mean it?"

"Why not?"

Delvigne still couldn't quite accept the idea.

"Of course we'd make it as comfortable as we could."

"No, no. That would spoil everything. No; you'll treat me exactly like anyone else."

"Your French methods are surprising."

"Not French methods. Just common sense. If you can't get the criminal rattled, put him at ease. The man who killed Graphopoulos will sleep better when he knows I'm sleeping in Saint-Léonard. Assuming, of course, that someone did kill him."

That was more than Delvigne could swallow.

"What do you mean? You're not suggesting that Graphopoulos bashed in his own skull, are you? And that he then stuffed himself into a wicker basket and had himself carted to the Zoo?"

Maigret's large eyes were artless as a child's as he murmured:

"One never knows. . . ."

Then, relighting his pipe, he went on more briskly:

"It's time you were packing me off to jail. Before I go, though, let's run through the principal points. You might jot them down, if you think it worthwhile. But don't leave your notes lying around."

Maigret spoke with the utmost simplicity. There was even a note of humility in his voice. That didn't alter the fact that he was nonetheless taking the case into his own hands and giving orders.

Delvigne did not demur.

"Fire away," he said.

"1. On Monday, Graphopoulos asks for police protection.

"2. He spends Tuesday trying to escape from it.

"3. On Wednesday, instead of flying to London, he takes a ticket for Berlin and detrains here.

"4. He seems to be a stranger in Liège, and there's nothing to show that he was led to the Gai-Moulin by anything but chance.

"5. When I leave with Adèle, he is still in the place, with four others: Génaro and Victor closing up for the night, Delfosse and Chabot hiding in the cellar.

"6. When I return, the place is shut and apparently lifeless.

"7. Chabot claims they left their hiding place a quarter of an hour after the Gai-Moulin closed, and that Graphopoulos was already lying dead on the floor.

"8. If Chabot is not telling the truth, there is no evidence that Graphopoulos was killed at the Gai-Moulin. Génaro and Victor swore he left, and there was no sign of his having broken in afterward.

"Have you checked that, by the way?"

"Yes. The place has been examined. No sign of a break-in. Or blood. Or burglary."

"And I understand that what Génaro, Victor, and Adèle say contradicts Chabot's story in almost every particular."

"So did Lasnier's evidence. He's Delfosse's uncle."

"That leaves us with two or three points to add.

"9. The next day, the boys have money, which Chabot tries to get rid of.

102

"10. Adèle has the gold cigarette case in her room, though she says Delfosse left it there.

"11. Delfosse runs away."

Maigret puffed at his pipe.

"I think that's about as far as we can go," he said after a few minutes. "What do you think?"

Delvigne's eyes were worried.

"It's unbelievable. . . ."

"What is?"

"The complexity of it all. The closer you look, the less you can make out."

Maigret stood up.

"Well, let's go to bed, anyhow. Are the beds nice and soft at Saint-Léonard?"

"You really do mean it?"

"By the way, will you put me in a cell next to young Chabot's? Perhaps tomorrow you'd like to confront him with me."

"In the meantime, we may have rounded up Delfosse."

"Oh . . . Delfosse."

"You don't believe the boys did it, do you?"

Maigret smoked thoughtfully without answering.

"The examining magistrate won't hear of my releasing Chabot, even on bail. . . . And, speaking of the examining magistrate, I'll have to tell him about you."

"I was afraid you would. But put it off as long as you can. . . . What's going on in the next room?"

"Reporters, I suppose. They're a noisy lot. They'll be wanting a statement. Who shall I say you are?"

"A stranger. A man with no papers who refuses to give his name. They can go on calling me the broad-shouldered man. It won't offend me at all!"

103

Inspector Delvigne was out of his depth. He eyed Maigret furtively, with a slightly uncomfortable admiration.

"I must confess," he said at last, "that I don't understand a thing."

"You know as much as I do."

"It's almost as if Graphopoulos came to Liège for the purpose of being killed. . . . That reminds me: I must inform the family. I'll see the Greek consul in the morning."

Maigret was standing, ready to go.

"Mind you're not too polite to me in front of the press," he said.

Delvigne opened the door, and both of them recognized the man who was standing in the big room surrounded by half a dozen reporters. It was the manager of the Hotel Moderne.

He was talking volubly while the others took notes. Catching sight of Maigret, he looked startled, and, pointing his finger, said:

"There he is! That's the man!"

"I know," said Delvigne. "He admits he stayed at your hotel."

"Does he admit taking the basket?"

Delvigne looked puzzled.

"What basket?"

"The wicker basket, of course. The one they found the body in. A fine lot of maids I've got! They only just told me about it."

"Would you mind explaining?"

"It's like this. On every landing there's a large wicker basket, which we use for linen. This afternoon the clean sheets came back from the laundry, and it was only then that someone noticed the second-floor basket was missing. As soon as I heard about it, I sent for the maid who does that floor. She said she thought it had been taken away to be fixed; one of the hinges was loose."

"Would it have been empty on Wednesday?"

"No. They're never quite empty. . . . We found the linen that had been in it in the basket on the next floor."

"How do you know it was that basket that was used for the corpse?"

"I rushed straight to the mortuary, where they showed it to me."

He was breathless, and furious. He couldn't get over his hotel's being mixed up in such a case. Even so, he wasn't half as upset as Delvigne, who didn't dare catch Maigret's eye. Forgetting all about the reporters and Maigret's warning, he said:

"What do you think about that?"

"I have nothing to say," answered Maigret stiffly.

"Of course," the manager rattled on, "he'd have had no difficulty at all in taking it out of the hotel without being seen—that is, at night. As a matter of fact, it's easy enough to get in. You just ring the bell, and the porter pulls the cord without leaving his bed. He's supposed to ask who it is, but usually he doesn't bother. And it's no use saying anything—they're all alike. . . . As for getting out, you don't even have to ring. You simply turn the handle and open the door yourself."

One of the reporters, who could sketch, was making a rapid portrait of Maigret in pencil. By somewhat exaggerating the line of the jaw, he made him look thoroughly villainous.

Delvigne ran his fingers through his hair, then stammered:

"Will you . . . just come back into my office a moment . . . ?"

He didn't know which way to turn, poor man. One of the reporters asked:

"Has he confessed?"

"Shut up," snapped Delvigne.

"I'm answering no questions," said Maigret quietly, "until I've seen a lawyer."

That decided Delvigne.

"Girard! Order a car."

"I suppose I'll have to sign a statement?" the manager said.

"All in good time!"

Delvigne snarled as questions were shot at him from all sides. Maigret was the only one to remain calm. Gravely smoking his pipe, he silently studied one after another of the faces around him.

"Handcuffs?" Girard asked as he came back into the room.

"Yes . . . No . . . Come along, you!"

Delvigne took Maigret's arm and hurried him away. He was longing to be alone in the car with him.

Lowering his voice so the driver wouldn't hear, he asked almost pathetically:

"What does this mean?"

"What?"

"This story about the basket. Why, the man prac-

tically accused you of having taken it from the hotel.
. . . The basket the body was found in!"

"I believe he was suggesting something of the
kind."

"Is it true?"

But Maigret would only tease him:

"To judge by appearances, it must have been
taken by Graphopoulos or me. And you'll admit that
it's very strange for a murder victim to carry his own
coffin."

"Excuse me, but . . ." Delvigne hesitated, coughed.
"But just now, when you told me who you were, I
didn't think of asking you for . . . of asking you to . . ."

Maigret plunged a hand into a pocket and brought
out his badge.

"Thank you . . . Forgive me . . . But this story of
the basket . . ."

Delvigne felt a little more at ease in the darkness
of the car, where he was immune to the burden of
Maigret's eye. Plucking up his courage, he went on:

"I suppose you realize that I'd have been obliged
to arrest you—policeman or not—after such an
accusation."

"Of course."

"Were you expecting it?"

"Me? . . . No."

"Then you think, after all, that Graphopoulos
must have taken it?"

"I think nothing at all—so far."

Delvigne was losing patience. He could feel the
blood mounting to his cheeks. Finally he decided to
give up, and the drive was finished in silence. At the

prison, he went through the formalities as quickly as possible, without once looking Maigret in the face.

"The warden will see to you."

That was all he said in farewell.

He was no sooner in the street, however, than he began to feel uncomfortable about it, wondering whether he hadn't been unnecessarily rude. Yet, after all, Maigret had asked him to . . .

"Exactly like anyone else."

Wasn't that how he'd asked to be treated? Still, it was different when they were alone.

Now, this wicker-basket story had added another aspect to things. . . . What was Maigret up to? Was he having a joke at the expense of the Belgian police? Did he think he could do as he liked, just because he came from Paris?

"If that's the case, he'll soon find out . . ." Delvigne muttered.

He found Girard waiting in his office—and reading, with a puzzled expression, the notes Maigret had particularly asked him not to leave lying around.

Not that it mattered much. Girard had to know. Even so, he was annoyed: annoyed with Girard, annoyed with himself, and, most of all, annoyed with Maigret.

"Call the post office," he rapped out irritably. "I want to send a telegram."

"When the phone was handed to him, he slowly dictated:

"Police Judiciaire Paris. Urgent please send detailed description Inspector Maigret. Sûreté Liège."

Girard's eyes opened wide. In spite of his chief's rasping voice, he couldn't help asking:

"Do you mean to say the fellow . . . that he's a policeman?"

Delvigne flared up.

"I didn't *mean* to say anything. But now you know, you'd better damn well keep it to yourself. And for heaven's sake clear out and leave me in peace."

So Delvigne was left in peace, or, to be more precise, was left wrathfully glaring at the sheet of paper on which Maigret's eleven points were set out.

Friends Confronted

"Don't be silly!" said the buxom young woman with a giggle. "People will see us."

She stood up, went over to the window, and looked out through the lace curtain. Then she asked:

"You're catching the Brussels train?"

It was a small café behind the Gare des Guillemins. The room, however, seemed spacious, and very clean, with a scrubbed tile floor and freshly varnished tables.

"Come and sit down," pleaded the man, who had a glass of beer in front of him.

"If you'll behave yourself."

She sat down again, took the man's straying hand, and planted it firmly on the table.

"You're a traveling salesman, aren't you?"

"What makes you think so?"

"I don't know. Nothing in particular . . . Now, look

here! If you want me to sit by you, you can keep your hands to yourself. And if you want to be sensible, you can order another drink."

"All right . . . Same again."

"Are you standing me one too?"

Perhaps it was the very cleanliness of the place that made it seem somewhat doubtful, made it seem a little more intimate than was proper in a public place.

The bar itself was tiny, and there was no sign of a beer spigot. On the shelf behind were only about twenty glasses. Some sewing had been left lying on a table by the window, and near it stood a basket of beans that someone had been stringing.

So spick and span, so homey. Was it surprising that the man was tempted to take liberties, to make himself too much at home?

The woman, who might be thirty-five, was attractive in a maternal way, and obviously a good soul. Cheerfully but inflexibly, she continued removing the hand, which persistently found its way back to her knee.

"What do you sell? Groceries?"

Suddenly she stopped to listen. Stairs led directly from the café to the next floor. From upstairs came the sound of someone moving.

"Just a moment . . ."

She went to the bottom of the stairs and listened. Then, disappearing into a passageway behind the bar, she called out:

"Monsieur Henri!"

When she returned to the salesman, she found him in a different mood, the hand no longer so ready for

111

adventure. And he was clearly ill at ease at the sight of the man in shirtsleeves who emerged from the passageway and quietly went upstairs.

"What is it?"

"Nothing. Just a young man who was drunk last night and had to be put to bed."

"And Monsieur Henri? Is he your husband?"

She burst into a loud, hearty laugh.

"He's the boss. I'm only the waitress. . . . Now don't start that again. I told you, they can see us from outside."

"You needn't be so standoffish. I only wanted . . ."

"Only wanted what?"

The man was confused. He couldn't figure out what was allowed and what wasn't. The shining eyes that leered at her seemed to want a good deal!

"A pity it's so public here."

"What are you thinking of? You're crazy. This is a respectable place. Whatever . . . ?"

She broke off, listening again, because a discussion had started on the floor above. The young man was ranting about something; Monsieur Henri was answering quietly and dryly.

"A mere boy," explained the woman. "Not yet twenty. And getting into such a state! I couldn't help feeling sorry for him. He was throwing his weight around, standing drinks all the time. And of course people took advantage of him."

The voices grew suddenly louder when a door upstairs was opened.

"I tell you, I had hundreds of francs in my pocket," the young man spluttered. "And they've been stolen. If I don't get them back, I'll . . ."

"Hold on there! There are no thieves in this place. If you hadn't been blind drunk . . ."

"You made me drunk on purpose!"

"When I give people drink, I assume they know how to hold it—and their money too. I shouldn't have had any truck with you. It would have served you right if I'd called the police. Hauling girls in from the street and trying to turn the place into a . . ."

"Give me back my money."

"I have not taken your money, and if you start making a row, you'll get more than you bargain for."

Monsieur Henri was cool as a cucumber, while the young man, shouting over his shoulder as he came down the stairs, became more and more incensed. His face was drawn, and there were dark shadows under his eyes.

"You're thieves! All of you!"

"Say that again!"

"A lousy bunch of thieves."

Then the sparks really began to fly. Monsieur Henri ran quickly down the last few steps and seized the boy by the collar. The latter whipped a gun out of his pocket.

"Take your dirty hands off me, or I'll . . ."

The salesman shrank back in his chair, nervously grabbing the waitress's arm as she made a move to jump up.

But there was no need for alarm. Monsieur Henri was perfectly capable of dealing with the situation. A quick jab at the boy's forearm, and the gun fell with a clatter to the tiles.

"Open the door," snapped Monsieur Henri to the waitress.

As soon as it was done, he gave his troublesome customer a shove that sent him sprawling full-length on the sidewalk. Then he picked up the gun and flung it after him.

"These young fools! They're enough to make you sick. One minute they're throwing their money around right and left, as if they had millions, and the next they come whining to you, saying they've been robbed."

He smoothed his hair, which had been slightly ruffled. Glancing out the door, he caught sight of a policeman.

"You saw what happened," he said to the salesman. "You can tell him he drew a gun on me. . . . But anyhow, the police know me."

Out on the sidewalk, René Delfosse, wild with fury, his teeth chattering, and hardly knowing what he was saying, was pouring out his story to the policeman.

"You say they've taken your money, do you? Well, first of all, who are you? Let's see your papers. And is that your gun on the ground there?"

People were gathering around. A streetcar passed the spot, and twenty heads inside it turned as one.

"I think you'd better come along with me, young man."

At the police station, Delfosse had to be dragged in, and the policeman's shins were badly kicked before the young man was finally hauled up before the divisional inspector.

The inspector had hardly opened his mouth when

114

Delfosse plunged into a story about being a Frenchman who had arrived in Liège the night before.

"I went straight from the station to that filthy café, where they first made me drunk and then stole everything, my money, my passport, and . . ."

One of the policemen present went to the chief and whispered two words in his ear. A quiet smile spread over the latter's face.

"Are you quite sure your name is not René Delfosse?"

The young man groped wildly for an answer.

"I . . . What? . . . That's none of your business."

They had rarely seen anybody so completely out of control. He was fuming. His features were twisted.

"And this money you say has been stolen—didn't it once belong to a certain dancer?"

"That's a lie."

"Take it easy, my boy. You can tell them all about it at the Sûreté. Here, you, call Inspector Delvigne and ask what we should do with him."

"I'm hungry," whined René.

Like a child in a tantrum, he was ready to say anything that came into his head.

Nobody was impressed.

"You have no right to refuse. I'll make a complaint. I've had nothing to eat since . . ."

"Oh, get him a sandwich, someone," said the inspector disgustedly.

After two bites, René threw the rest on the floor.

"Hello! . . . Delvigne? . . . He's here. . . . Yes, I'll send him over at once. . . . No. Nothing so far."

Driving to the Sûreté, wedged between two policemen, René was obstinately silent, until suddenly he volunteered:

"I didn't do it. It was Chabot."

His escort made no response.

"My father will complain to the governor, who's a friend of his. . . . I've done nothing at all. . . . My money was stolen, and they wanted to turn me out into the street without a sou."

"So you drew your gun."

"It wasn't my gun. It was his. He threatened to shoot if I made a fuss. There was a man sitting in the café—you can ask him."

As they entered the Sûreté, he straightened up, trying to look cool and collected, like a person of some social standing. They were met by a detective, who shook hands with the escort, and then looked René over.

"So you've nabbed him! I'll let the chief know."

He returned a moment later to say:

"He can wait."

The boy's face fell, and his air of superiority melted into one of strained anxiety. He wanted to smoke, but they wouldn't let him.

"It's not allowed."

"But *you're* smoking!"

That was quite true. Around him, almost everyone was smoking as they bent over their work, checking criminal records or making copies of statements. Now and then a few casual remarks were exchanged.

But the protest fell on deaf ears. René heard one of them mutter:

"A comic little fighting cock!"

A bell rang.

"You can go in now. Door at the end."

The inspector's room was small, and the air was blue with tobacco smoke. The stove, which had been lighted for the first time that autumn, roared with each gust of wind.

Delvigne leaned back in his chair. Near the window someone else was sitting, against the light.

"Come in. . . . Sit down."

The silhouette in front of the window straightened. Jean Chabot's pale face was just visible as he turned toward his friend.

"What do you want me for?" René began, aggressively.

"Oh, nothing much," answered Delvigne. "I'd merely like to ask you a few questions."

"I haven't done anything."

"I never said you had."

Looking toward Jean, René said sourly:

"What's he been telling you? I know he's been lying."

"Now, now! Just answer my questions." Then to Chabot: "As for you, you keep quiet."

"But . . ."

"*You keep quiet;* that's what I said. And now, young Delfosse, tell me what you were doing in this café— what's it called?—Chez Jeanne."

"They stole my money there."

"Begin at the beginning. . . . You arrived there in the afternoon and you were already none too sober. You wanted to take the waitress upstairs, and when she refused, you dragged some girls in from the street."

"They came on their own. I didn't force them."

117

"You stood round after round of drinks, playing the millionaire, until you finally rolled, dead-drunk, under the table. They took pity on you, and dumped you on one of the beds upstairs."

"They stole my money."

"You'd been throwing it away the whole evening. *Your* money indeed! You mean the money you took yesterday morning from Adèle Bosquet's bag."

"That's not true."

"The first thing you bought with it was a gun. . . . What did you want that for?"

"I just thought I'd like one."

Jean was a fascinating study. He looked at his friend with utter bewilderment, as though he could hardly believe his ears. This was a Delfosse he had never seen before, a Delfosse who was positively frightening. If only he could talk to him, could tell him to be careful, to speak the truth. . . .

"Why did you take Adèle's money?"

"She gave it to me."

"That's not her version."

"Then she's lying. She gave it to me to buy our tickets. We were going away together."

He was still saying anything that crossed his mind, not caring what it was or how often he contradicted himself.

"Perhaps you'll also deny hiding in the cellar of the Gai-Moulin."

Jean was straining forward in his chair, as though longing to come to the rescue, to warn his friend:

"Be careful what you say. It's no use lying. I *had* to tell them."

But René had sprung to his feet and was shouting.

"He told you that too, did he? There's not a word of truth in it. He wanted me to, but I wouldn't listen. Why should I? I don't want money! My father's got plenty, and I only have to ask for it. The whole thing was his idea. But I wasn't playing."

"So you left right away?"

"Yes."

"And went home?"

"Yes."

"After having some mussels and fried potatoes on Rue du Pont d'Avroy?"

"Yes . . . At least . . . I think . . ."

"The waiter there says you were with Chabot."

Jean was wringing his hands. His look was supplicating.

"Even so, I didn't do anything." René hammered the words out.

"Who said you did?"

"Then what about it?"

"Nothing about it."

René took a deep breath. He looked shiftily from the inspector to Jean.

"You pushed Chabot in front of you when you left the cellar. . . ."

"That's not true."

"You struck a match, and it was you who saw the body."

"That's not true."

"René! . . . Please! . . ."

Jean had risen from his chair. He simply couldn't keep the words back. The inspector tried to shut him up, but the boy stumbled on desperately.

"I don't know why he talks like that. There's no

need to lie. We didn't kill anybody. We didn't even have time to look for the money. . . . I was in front. But I couldn't see. I asked him for a light. He struck a match. . . . And there, lying on the floor . . . I hardly saw it. . . . But he did. He even noticed one eye was open. He said so afterward. . . ."

René jeered:

"You don't say!"

At that moment Jean looked a full five years younger than his friend. A mere boy. He looked helpless, daunted by his friend's brazenness.

Delvigne looked at them.

"Come, children! Don't quarrel! . . . The two of you left the place in such a hurry that you didn't even remember to shut the door. Then you had a meal together on Rue du Pont d'Avroy."

Then suddenly, looking into René's eyes, he asked:

"By the way, did you touch the body?"

"*Me?* . . . Never!"

"You didn't see a wicker basket there?"

"No."

"How many times have you pinched money from your uncle's till?"

"Chabot said that?"

And, clenching his fists:

"The little swine! He's got some nerve. Because he takes money from the petty cash, he thinks other people are just the same. . . . I was the one who gave him money to pay it back with."

"Stop! Stop! Please!" Jean pleaded.

"You know you're lying. You . . ."

"Why don't you tell the truth? Listen, René. The murderer's been . . ."

120

"What?"

"The murderer's been . . . been arrested. You're only making things worse by . . ."

René turned to Delvigne, asking in a puzzled voice:

"What's he talking about? The . . . murderer . . ."

"Haven't you heard? Well, I have a man here, and I want you to tell me if you recognize him. He seems to have been at the Gai-Moulin on Wednesday and to have followed you next day."

René wiped his forehead. He didn't dare look at Jean.

A bell rang in the next room. A minute or two later the door opened, and Maigret was ushered in by Girard.

"Come on! Step over here, will you? . . . Face to the light . . . Now, Delfosse, do you recognize him?"

"That's the man."

"You never saw him before that night?"

"Never."

"Did he speak to you?"

"I don't think so."

"When you left the Gai-Moulin, you didn't see him hanging around? Think carefully before you answer."

"Wait a minute. I think maybe there was . . . Yes. I remember now. There was someone standing in the shadow by the wall. It might have been him."

"Might have been?"

"Yes. I'm sure. It was."

In the little room, Maigret looked enormous. Yet when he spoke, it was in a gentle, almost fragile voice.

"Have you got a flashlight?"

"No. Why?"

121

"So it was only by the light of a match that you saw the body? How far away were you?"

"It's hard to say."

"As far as from one wall to the other of this room?"

"Maybe . . . About that."

"Then it wasn't less than twelve feet. I suppose you'd never burgled a place before?"

"Never."

"So you might have been excited. And seeing a man on the floor, you jumped to the conclusion it was a corpse. . . . You didn't go up to it, did you?"

"No."

"Who held the match?"

"I did."

"How long did it burn?"

"I dropped it almost right away."

"So this corpse was only lighted up for a matter of seconds. . . . You're sure it was Graphopoulos?"

"I could see his curly black hair."

"But you couldn't swear he wasn't still breathing?"

"I . . ."

René bridled. He had suddenly realized that the man was cross-examining him. In a sullen voice he growled:

"You can keep your questions to yourself. I'll only answer the inspector."

The latter had picked up the telephone. René winced when he heard the number he asked for.

"Hello! Is this Monsieur Delfosse? . . . About the question of bail, I've spoken to the examining magistrate, and he's had a word with the public prosecutor. . . . Yes. . . . If you're willing to put down fifty thousand francs, I think it'll be all right. . . . No, you needn't bother. I'll go myself and arrange it."

René had not yet quite grasped the situation. In his chair by the window, Jean sat motionless.

"You still maintain that it's all Chabot's fault?"

"Everything."

"Very well! You'll be released now, and you'd better go home. Your father's ready to make things easy for you. . . . As for you, Chabot, you still say the money you wanted to throw away was what Delfosse took from his uncle's shop."

"That's what he told me."

"Well, you can thrash that out between you. Run along, the pair of you. And keep out of trouble."

Unthinkingly, Maigret had taken his pipe out of his pocket. But he quickly slipped it back again. He studied the boys, who were standing awkwardly, not knowing what to do with themselves or which way to look. Delvigne had to get up from his chair and push them out of the room.

"Don't forget you're still at the disposal of the police. You may be wanted again. . . . And don't start quarreling."

They walked off rapidly, but before they were out of sight, René had turned furiously on his friend. His words were not audible, but they were certainly the most wounding he could find.

The inspector was at the telephone again.

"Yes. Delvigne speaking."

"I'm Jean Chabot's father. Forgive my bothering

you, Inspector. I wondered if you could give me any news."

Delvigne smiled, put his meerschaum pipe down on the table, and gave Maigret a wink.

"Your son has just left, accompanied by René Delfosse."

"What!"

"He's been released. You'll have him home in a few minutes. . . . Are you there? . . . Just one thing: if you take my advice, you'll let him off lightly."

It was raining. Jean and René walked fast, threading their way through crowds that were quite unconscious of them. They were not exactly talking, nor were they silent. About every hundred yards or so, one of them would turn his head slightly toward the other to make some biting remark, which was answered no less bitingly.

At the corner of Rue Puits-en-Soc they branched off, one to the right, the other to the left, toward their respective homes.

"He's been released, monsieur. They've declared him innocent."

Monsieur Chabot left his office, waited for a Number 4 streetcar, and, when it came, climbed up beside the driver, with whom he had been friendly for years.

"Be careful now! Don't run into anything, because I'm in a hurry. My son's been released! The inspector's just telephoned to say it was all a mistake."

It was difficult to know whether he was laughing or crying. In any case, there was a mist before his eyes, which prevented his seeing anything very clearly.

124

"With any luck, I'll be home before he is. Better if I am. His mother might not welcome him in the right way. There are some things women don't understand. . . . Did you believe for a moment he was capable of doing such a thing? Honestly?"

He was touching. Every line of his body was begging the driver to say no.

"I don't set myself up as a judge. . . ."

"But you must have had an opinion."

"I don't set myself up as a judge. . . . But I must say, ever since my daughter went and married a good-for-nothing who'd got her in a family way, I haven't thought very highly of the young people of today."

Meanwhile, Maigret had sunk into the chair Jean Chabot had vacated. Leaning forward, he stretched a hand toward Delvigne's desk and helped himself to some tobacco.

"Have you had an answer from Paris?"

"How did you know . . . ?"

Maigret grinned.

"I'd have done the same in your place. So would anybody. . . . That wicker basket—have you managed to find out how it was removed from the Moderne?"

"No, I haven't," grunted Delvigne, who was still feeling sore on that subject. "Between ourselves, aren't you having a little joke at our expense? You have something up your sleeve, don't you?"

"The mystery isn't solved, no. We're both in the dark. . . . But I think you did right to release those youngsters. What we ought to find out now is what

125

Graphopoulos could have been stealing from the Gai-Moulin."

"Stealing?"

"Or trying to steal."

"Graphopoulos?"

"Or who he could have been trying to kill."

"You see! You *do* know something. You *are* holding something back."

"Not much. The chief difference between us is that you've been up to your eyes in work, running here and there, telephoning, questioning people; whereas I've had plenty of time for quiet meditation in my cell at Saint-Léonard."

"You've been thinking over your eleven points?"

There was a touch of pique in Delvigne's voice.

"Some of them. Not all."

"And wondering about the basket?"

Maigret's grin was broader than ever.

"Still harping on that? . . . All right, old friend, I'll tell you. *I* took it from the hotel."

"Empty?"

"Good God, no! With a corpse in it!"

"So the fact is . . ."

"That the murder was committed at the Moderne. That's the problem. . . . Toss me the matches, will you?"

—9—

A Suicide

It was evident that Delvigne was uncertain what posture to take. Should he be grateful for the information? Or was he entitled to resentment and indignation? After all, this was almost too much.

Maigret leaned back in his chair. He hesitated, as he generally did before embarking on a long explanation, wondering how to put it in the simplest and most convincing way.

"I think you'll understand," he began at last, "and I hope you'll forgive me if you think I haven't played fair with you. But there was no use throwing suspicion on me unless we did it thoroughly, and it's not always easy to fool the press. Some of them will swallow anything, but others are just as clever as we are.

"By keeping something back, I helped you play your part. More than you realize. You should have seen your face when the manager of the Moderne told you about the basket! You never could have looked like that on purpose—not to save your life. It did the trick, more than anything."

The scowl on Delvigne's face relaxed a trifle.

"And now," Maigret went on, "let's put our heads together and see what we can make of this business.

"Let's start again at the Paris end. First, Graphopoulos asks for protection, then seems to regret it. What could be the explanation for that?

"He might be crazy. Some queer form of persecution mania that comes over him in fits and starts.

"Second, his life may really be threatened for some reason he doesn't dare explain. Then the danger passes, and he wants to fade away quietly. Or perhaps he changes his mind and feels that the presence of the police only makes matters worse.

"Third, he's simply making use of the police for some special purpose of his own.

"Here's a man in the prime of life, with plenty of money, free to go anywhere and do whatever he likes. From what direction is his life likely to be threatened? A jealous woman out for vengeance? I hardly think so. He has only to take the first train or plane he fancies and put a thousand miles between himself and her. Besides, if that was the reason, why shouldn't he tell me?

"He's a banker's son whose name is well known to the embassy people. His shoulders ought to be broad enough, therefore, to enable him to stand up to any personal enemy. He can hardly have a business enemy, since he's never done a stroke of work in his life. If someone had been demanding money as a bribe for silence, he might have been afraid to go to the police at all. But, having gone, surely he'd have told the whole story.

"It occurred to me then that he might be afraid not of a person but of some organization, an international organization that wouldn't be so easy to escape from.

"He was afraid in Paris. He was afraid on the train—I'm quite sure of that. He was certainly uneasy at the Gai-Moulin. Whatever the danger was, it apparently followed him everywhere. . . . Exactly as though he were a member of some secret society and been condemned to death for some act of betrayal. Like the Mafia, for instance, or a band of international spies. There are any number of Greeks in the world of spying.

"He might not even have betrayed anybody. He might simply be sick of the spying business and have announced his intention of retiring. His confederates aren't ready to let him go, and they swear that, if he does, they'll have his blood sooner or later. He comes to me, but I've no sooner done what he asks than he jumps to the conclusion that it won't serve any purpose. . . .

"Or it might be just the other way around."

"What do you mean? I don't follow."

"Graphopoulos is rich and idle. He has no ties or responsibilities of any kind. He's a spoiled boy, and spoiled boys never find life amusing enough. In search of new excitement he joins some secret organization, to which he swears absolute obedience. Then one day he's given a job to do—possibly to kill somebody."

"And he goes to the police?"

"Wait! . . . Let's say, for instance, that he's told to

kill somebody in Liège. He entered the gang light-heartedly enough, but he suddenly realizes what he's in—and wants to back out. Yet he doesn't dare refuse. So what does he do?

"Rather ingeniously, he arranges for a detective to follow him day and night. Then he reports to his boss that the police are on his trail, and suggests that someone else will have to do the job.

"But the boss isn't having this. He tells him to go through with it just the same. So, after trying to shake us off, Graphopoulos comes here to carry out his orders, and, tackling the job halfheartedly, gets killed instead of killing."

"Unless, of course," Delvigne put in, "he came to Liège not to do a job but to escape from doing it. In that case, his death would be revenge."

"A few hours after getting here! Rather too soon for revenge. If he was killed in revenge, it's more likely he was sent here on some apparently harmless errand, but really to walk into a trap."

"And also, as you said yourself, he might have been crazy."

"But who wants to kill a lunatic?"

"True . . . It's complicated." Delvigne sighed.

For a while, there was no sound except the wheezing of Maigret's pipe. Then he began again:

"To get on with the story: on Wednesday night, Graphopoulos goes to the Gai-Moulin, where Adèle looks after him. When the place shuts, I lose track of him and, after checking the other nightclubs, I return to the hotel, about four in the morning.

"The key for Number 18 is hanging on the board;

so apparently he hasn't come back. It seems a good opportunity to have a look at his room. I take the key and go in. . . ."

Maigret leaned forward in his chair.

"And there was the body, fully dressed, at the foot of the bed, with the skull bashed in. The man's wallet was gone, and I could find nothing in the room that offered any clue at all. If I'd called you in then, what would you have had to go on?"

Maigret did not wait for Delvigne to answer the question.

"It had already occurred to me that some international organization might be behind the man's strange behavior. The murder made it seem even more likely. Judging by the absence of clues, it looked like a professional job. You might have found fingerprints, of course, but I felt almost certain you wouldn't. It looked like the work of people who'd taken every precaution.

"It was just because it seemed to have been such a perfect job that I thought I'd make a mess of it— draw a red herring across the trail, to set them guessing, make them jumpy. They'd left the body in the Moderne, had they? Well, it would give them a jolt if it was found in quite a different place. So I shoved it unceremoniously into the basket that was on the landing outside and dragged it downstairs as quietly as I could."

"How did you get it to the Zoo?"

"In a taxi. The driver helped me carry it to the lawn."

"He wasn't suspicious?"

"Very! But I made up an excuse, and when I gave him a hundred francs, he pretended to believe it. He hasn't come forward, I suppose?"

"I should think not!"

"So a few hours later the body was duly discovered, crammed tight in a wicker basket on a public lawn. Think of the murderer's face! Better still, the faces of his accomplices! Would they believe the murderer's story? Wouldn't they think there was something fishy about it, maybe some double-crossing going on? Wouldn't it throw them all into confusion? Perhaps induce them to give each other away?

"But they weren't the only ones to get a surprise. You can imagine my face when I read in the papers that Jean Chabot swore that he and his friend had seen the body at the Gai-Moulin a quarter of an hour after the place shut!"

"I'm inclined to think he's telling the truth."

"I don't say he's lying. But they might have been mistaken. Chabot saw almost nothing, and Delfosse caught the merest glimpse of the body—one eye open—before he dropped his match. They were in no state to make accurate observations, were they? Their first crime! They'd been waiting for half an hour on the cellar steps, and I bet their teeth were chattering.

"Particularly Delfosse—I've no doubt he was the ringleader, and I'd guess his nerves are shot at the best of times. Look at his face! Bad health, no stamina, no morals of any description. But imagination—yes. And seeing Graphopoulos stretched out on the floor—it wouldn't take him a fraction of a second to jump to conclusions.

"He was too scared to go up and touch him. He

didn't light another match. No thought of the cashbox now. They both simply turned tail and fled. So we'd better regard their evidence with the utmost skepticism—on this point at any rate.

"As I said just now, what we want to find out is what Graphopoulos could have been up to in the Gai-Moulin after it was closed."

Maigret looked at Delvigne, but it was difficult to guess what the inspector was thinking.

"We can rule out jealousy and hatred as motives for this crime," he continued. "And although his money's gone, I can't bring myself to believe that's at the bottom of it. To my mind, it's the kind of crime the police rarely manage to clear up, because it's been committed by people too experienced and too well organized.

"That's why a routine investigation seemed only too likely to give negative results. By removing the body, I must have puzzled them. The next thing to do was to throw them off guard. That's why I insisted that you arrest me. Let them think you're off on a wild-goose chase. They may relax and make a slip."

Delvigne was listening attentively. What was he to make of this somewhat lurid story? He hadn't quite forgiven Maigret, and a frown still hovered on his forehead.

Maigret looked at him coaxingly, then broke into a hearty laugh.

"Come on, old friend! Don't be too hard on me. If I did hold something back, that only made things even. Because there's one thing you knew and I didn't. In fact, I don't know it yet."

"What's that?"

133

"The basket was discovered Thursday morning. And the only clue to the dead man's identity was a card with his name on it, no address. Yet the same afternoon you were at the Gai-Moulin, and on the track of the two boys. Who put you on *their* trail?"

Delvigne smiled. Certainly he was to windward of Maigret there, and he thoroughly relished it. Instead of answering at once, he lighted his pipe, taking his time about it.

"Of course," he said vaguely, "I have my informers. . . ."

He fidgeted to prolong the moment, even gathering together a few papers that were lying on his desk.

"I suppose you do things pretty much the same way in Paris. The owners of almost all the clubs play into our hands, in return for which we wink at minor breaches of the regulations."

"So it was Génaro?"

Delvigne nodded.

"Génaro came to tell you that Graphopoulos had spent the evening at the Gai-Moulin?"

"Yes. He came soon after the newspapers were out."

"And he told you about the cigarette butts on the cellar steps?"

"Victor had called his attention to them. He just asked me to come and see for myself."

The Belgian had recovered his good humor, perhaps all the more readily because it was now Maigret's turn to look glum.

"We certainly didn't lose much time. . . . But you don't seem pleased about this."

134

"It doesn't make things simpler."

"What doesn't?"

"Génaro's coming to you like that."

"You've had your eye on him, haven't you? You fancy him as the murderer?"

"Not him particularly. And this action of his doesn't prove anything one way or the other. At the most, it shows he's very sure of himself."

"Do you want to go back to prison, then?"

Maigret was fiddling with the box of matches. He seemed in no hurry to answer, and when he did speak, it was more to himself than to his listener.

"Graphopoulos came to Liège to kill somebody . . . or to be killed."

"That's not really certain."

Suddenly Maigret burst out angrily:

"Those wretched boys!"

"What do you mean?"

"Those wretched boys, who went and spoiled everything . . . Unless . . ."

"Unless what?"

"Nothing . . ."

He stood up and began pacing impatiently.

"Still," said Delvigne, "if you'd left the body where it was, and we'd made a thorough investigation, we might have . . ."

Maigret glared at him.

Delvigne's good humor was short-lived, and both of them were now in a bad temper. They knew they were making no headway, and were each ready to think it was the other's fault. It wouldn't have taken much to start a real quarrel.

"Haven't you got any tobacco?"

Maigret asked the question in exactly the same tone he'd have used if he'd said:

"Of all the fools I've ever met . . ."

He took the pouch that was handed him and filled his pipe. His hand then moved absentmindedly toward his pocket.

"Hey, that's mine! You can't go stealing on these premises!"

Delvigne spoke gruffly, but with an undertone of banter that sufficed to clear the air. The crisis was over. Maigret looked down at the pouch, then at his companion, and a shamefaced grin spread over his features.

Delvigne grinned back. It was all right now. The breach was mended, though for form's sake they wouldn't unbend too quickly.

They felt embarrassed. To avoid an awkward silence, Delvigne asked:

"Well, what conclusions are we to come to?"

"I'm afraid there's nothing we can conclude, except that Graphopoulos was killed."

"At the hotel?"

"Yes, at the hotel, whoever did it: Génaro, Victor, Adèle, or one of the boys. They haven't one really good alibi among them. By the way, what's yours?"

"I was sleeping in my bed, monsieur, while you were carousing around the nightclubs!"

The witticism may have been a little forced, but it served to put them at ease.

"One thing's certain," said Maigret seriously, "and that is that Graphopoulos was in the Gai-Moulin for no legitimate reason. When he was disturbed, he could think of nothing better to do than to lie down and pretend to be dead. And, thanks to the boys being in a state of terror, it worked perfectly. Poor fellow! He didn't know he'd be acting the same part a great deal more realistically an hour or two later."

A hurried knock on the door, and one of the detectives entered.

"It's Monsieur Chabot. He says, if you're not too busy, he'd like to have a couple of words with you."

The two inspectors exchanged glances.

"All right," said Delvigne, "show him in." And to Maigret: "You'd better hide that pipe. . . . And don't look as though you'd bought the place!"

Maigret smiled, slipped his pipe in his pocket, and tried to look harassed.

Monsieur Chabot became even more uncomfortable when he found that Delvigne was not alone. He fidgeted, then finally said:

"I'm afraid I'm disturbing you."

"You have something to tell me?"

The inspector's voice was so businesslike, the question did not help the man at all.

"That is . . . I'm sorry if I'm bothering you. I only wanted . . . wanted to thank you for . . . ."

"Your son's at home?"

"He's been home this last hour. . . . He told me . . ."

"What did he tell you?"

It was pitiful. Monsieur Chabot became more and more disconcerted. He had come with such good intentions, but these blunt questions threw him off balance, and he quite forgot the speech he had prepared.

It was a poor, touching little speech that might have sounded all right with a little encouragement. Now, it was a jumble in his mind.

"He told me . . . At least . . . I wanted to thank you for being so kind. . . . You know, he's not really a bad boy at all. Only, getting into bad company, and perhaps not being quite as strong-willed as he should be . . . He swears . . . His mother's in bed, and it was at her side that he swore he'd . . . Really, Inspector, I can assure you you'll never have any trouble with him again. . . . You're convinced of his innocence, aren't you?"

The accountant had a lump in his throat. He was making a tremendous effort to keep his self-possession.

"He's my only son, and . . . But I suppose I've been too easy on him."

"Much too easy!"

Monsieur Chabot was rapidly losing what little composure was left to him. Maigret turned his head away, afraid the man was going to break down altogether—this narrow-shouldered, forty-five-year-old man with meticulous hair and mustache.

"I promise, for the future . . ."

Unable to complete the sentence, he asked:

"Do you think I ought to write to the examining magistrate to thank him?"

"By all means! By all means!" Delvigne said, standing up. "It's an excellent idea."

And he held out his hand to Monsieur Chabot, who backed out of the room, bowing as he went.

"Somehow, I don't think Delfosse's father will come to thank us," muttered Delvigne as soon as the door was closed. "But then, of course, *he* dines once a week with the provincial governor, and he's hail-fellow-well-met with the public prosecutor."

Then, with a heavy sigh and a look of disgust:

"Well, let's get on with the job. . . . What are we going to do?"

At that moment Adèle was no doubt still sleeping in her untidy room. At the Gai-Moulin, Victor and Joseph would be lazily wiping the marble-topped tables and polishing the mirrors.

Another knock on the door.

"Someone to see you from the *Gazette de Liège*. Says you promised to . . ."

"Let him wait."

Maigret had returned to his chair and was staring gloomily in front of him.

"That's an idea . . ." he muttered at last. "What's he like?"

"Who?"

"This newspaperman. *Gazette de Liège*. A nice gullible fellow?"

"He always prints what we tell him."

"The men in the next room—do they know about me?"

"Yes. They all know."

"And I suppose you can trust them?"

"Absolutely."

"Good . . . Hand me your gun. . . . It's all right. I'm not going to kill anybody. I'm just going to fire a shot in the air. Then you dash into the next room, before anybody can come in. Say I shot myself, having realized the game was up. Talk as though that settled everything, and the case would now be closed. Then get rid of him as quick as you can. I don't suppose he'll want to stay; he'll just be in time for the first afternoon edition. . . . As soon as he's gone, explain

139

things to your men. Then we'll map out our campaign."

"But . . ."

"Stand by! . . . Here goes!"

Maigret had shifted his chair over behind the door. Sitting in it, still puffing at his pipe, he fired.

Silence in the next room. Then a scurry of feet toward the chief's office. But the inspector met his men at the door, blocking the way.

"It's all right," he called out. "Nothing to worry about. He's shot himself. . . ."

"Who is it?" asked the man from the *Gazette de Liège*.

"The broad-shouldered Frenchman."

"He confessed?"

"That's about what it comes to. I had him cornered, and . . ."

He moved into the other room and shut the door behind him, leaving Maigret hunched in his chair, gazing glumly out the window. Running his fingers through his hair, he muttered to himself, reciting like a litany:

"Adèle . . . Génaro . . . Victor . . . Delfosse . . . Chabot . . ."

Meanwhile, the reporter was hurriedly scribbling notes.

"So there's no doubt about it? . . . You still have no clue to his identity? . . . Well, maybe you'll have more information later. I've got to catch the Bourse edition."

The moment he'd gone, a cheery voice piped up:

"Hey, Chief! The pipes have arrived. Would you like to choose yours?"

140

Delvigne stood there, playing with his mustache. He wasn't in the mood to choose anything.

"Later," he grunted.

"And they work out two francs apiece cheaper than I told you."

"Oh, yes?"

His real train of thought was betrayed by what he muttered under his breath:

". . . talking about the Mafia . . ."

10

A Scuffle in the Dark

"You're sure of your men?"

"I'm sure of one thing: nobody'll guess they're police. And that's for the simple reason that they're not. At the Gai-Moulin I've stationed my brother-in-law, who's spending a couple of days in Liège. He lives in Spa, and nobody knows him here. The other one is a tax clerk. I asked him for the special purpose of keeping an eye on Adèle. The real police are in the background."

The night was cold, and the asphalt glistened under fine rain. Maigret, officially dead, had been smuggled discreetly out of the Sûreté, his coat collar turned up and a muffler hiding half his face. He now stood with Delvigne in a dark street off well-lighted Rue du Pot d'Or. They could see, a little way down, the bright sign of the Gai-Moulin.

Delvigne, being still in the land of the living, was

142

not obliged to be so careful. He had imprudently left his overcoat behind, and was now muttering imprecations against the rain he hadn't bargained for.

Their watch had started at eight-thirty, before the doors of the nightclub were opened. They had seen its employees arrive one after another—Victor a good first, then Joseph, then Génaro.

The proprietor had switched on the electric sign just as the first of the musicians was rounding the corner of Rue du Pont d'Avroy.

On the stroke of nine the band struck up, and Joseph took up a stand at the entrance, counting the change he had in his pocket. A few minutes later the first customer arrived, none other than Delvigne's brother-in-law, followed shortly after by the tax clerk.

Delvigne recapitulated the strategic situation:

"There are two men in the alley behind, so nobody can slip out that way. Another two are covering the front and back entrances of Adèle's place on Rue de la Régence. Besides that, four other houses are being watched: Delfosse's, Chabot's, Génaro's, and Victor's. And there's a man in the Hotel Moderne."

Maigret said nothing. As a matter of fact, the whole plan was his. His suicide had been announced that afternoon by the *Gazette de Liège*, and in their later editions the other papers had picked it up. It was understood that the case was just about closed.

"Before the night's out," Maigret had said to his colleagues, "the murderer and his accomplices may fall into our hands. If not, I think we'll go on groping in the dark for months."

The afternoon had dragged on slowly at the Sûreté; Maigret walked up and down, up and down, smoking incessantly, his shoulders hunched. Delvigne had attempted conversation, if only to pass the time. But he got little response from his companion beyond an occasional grunt.

Once, he'd asked:

"We're hoping for something to happen, yes. But from what direction do you expect it to come?"

The only answer had been a blank stare.

It was nearly ten o'clock when Adèle arrived, followed at a distance by one of the Sûreté men. As she went in, the man walked casually past his chief and quietly threw him a word:

"Nothing!"

In the distance they could see Rue du Pont d'Avroy, which was brilliantly lighted. A streetcar passed every two or three minutes, and in spite of the rain, a constant stream of people flowed by on the sidewalks.

It was the traditional thing to do in Liège in the evening—a stroll along Rue du Pont d'Avroy. Old people, youngsters, whole families, saucy girls arm in arm, noisy young men. There were casual poor people, stiff and starched rich people.

In the side streets were the nightclubs, shady haunts like the Gai-Moulin. There were dark figures against walls, women walking up and down. . . .

"Have you really any hope?"

But Maigret only shrugged, and his eyes were so utterly mild they seemed devoid of intelligence.

"Anyhow, I don't think we'll find Master Chabot roaming around tonight. He won't so much as stir from his mother's bedside."

Delvigne couldn't resign himself to silence. He looked at his new pipe from the factory in Arlon.

"You must remind me tomorrow to give you one. A little memento of Liège."

Two men walked into the Gai-Moulin.

"We know them both. They're regular customers. One's a tailor on Rue Hors-Château, the other has a garage. A pair of night birds."

Maigret stood with his hands deep in his pockets. Without seeming to look at anything, he was taking in every detail, every passerby. It was he who first spotted René Delfosse's weedy figure and scraggy neck as he came around a corner into Rue du Pot d'Or. René crossed over to the opposite sidewalk, hesitated, went on, then once more crossed the street. He too was being discreetly shadowed by one of Delvigne's men. After hesitating again, the boy hurried toward the Gai-Moulin and went in.

"So he's off on a spree again!" said Delvigne.

"You think?"

"What?"

"Nothing!"

But if Maigret had nothing to say, his curiosity had nevertheless been aroused. He was no longer quite so mild. Creeping forward, he even ventured unwittingly within range of a streetlight, which revealed the upper part of his face.

He quickly drew back, however, when René reappeared, after barely ten minutes.

"Well . . ." Delvigne said, "what's he up to now?"

Maigret sighed and frowned. Really—this Belgian . . . Couldn't he keep his mouth shut for a minute?

The boy's gait was no longer undecided as he strode toward Rue du Pont d'Avroy. Before he was out of sight, Delvigne's brother-in-law came out to the sidewalk and peered right and left into the darkness. Delvigne had to give him a low whistle.

"Well?"

"Delfosse sat down next to Adèle and began talking seriously, in a whisper. He seemed to be begging for something. Finally—I can't be sure—she handed him something. His hand went to his pocket as he stood up. Then he hurried out."

"Did he speak to Victor?" asked Maigret.

"No, but Victor seemed to be keeping an eye on him. And as soon as Delfosse left, he spoke to Adèle. . . . Do you want me to stay there?"

"Yes. Of course . . . Stroll in as though you'd just been out for a breath of fresh air."

Before he reached the entrance, another man came out. Victor. He had discarded his apron and slipped on his coat. He too walked quickly toward Rue du Pont d'Avroy.

"What on earth . . . ?" began Delvigne, but the rest of the sentence was jolted out of his mind when Maigret seized him by the arm and dragged him around the corner into Rue du Pot d'Or.

"Are we going to follow him?"

"Yes. To Adèle's . . . René asked her for her key. Victor's after him."

On Rue du Pont d'Avroy they lost sight of Victor in the crowd, but as soon as they turned into Rue de la Régence they saw his dark figure hurrying along, then disappearing through the doorway of Adèle's building.

"What do we do now?"

"Just a minute. Where's your man?"

Girard was approaching, looking questioningly at his chief as he wondered whether he should speak to him or pretend not to know him.

"Well, Girard? What's going on?"

"Five minutes ago Delfosse went in. Now and then there was a glimmer of light in Adèle's room, as though he was using a flashlight."

"Come!" Maigret said.

"We're going in?"

"We certainly are!"

There was no light on the stairs, and no slit of light under Adèle's door. But when Maigret touched the door, it opened at once. Inside, a dull scuffle was heard, as though two people were wrestling on the floor.

Delvigne was holding his gun. Maigret felt for the switch by the door, and a second later the room was bathed in light, revealing an ugly, but nonetheless comic sight.

It was just what it had sounded like. Rolling on the floor René and Victor were at each other's throats. The light startled them, and, still locked in each other's arms, they lay motionless.

"Stand up!" ordered Delvigne. "And put your hands up."

Covering them with his gun, he shut the door behind him. Meanwhile, Maigret, with a sigh of relief, was unwinding his muffler and unbuttoning his coat. Once again he sighed, like a man who's been too hot and can at last breathe freely.

"Get a move on! Hands up, I said."

But they were so entwined that Victor, as he rose to his feet, tripped René, and the boy fell down again.

What was the next step? Delvigne's eye sought Maigret's. René and the waiter were standing now, pale, disheveled, crestfallen.

Of the two, the boy was in a much sorrier plight. He seemed quite unable to figure out what was going on. He gaped at Victor as if astonished to see him there.

Who had he imagined he was fighting with? A policeman?

"That's right," said Maigret, opening his mouth at last, "both of you keep still."

Moving over to Delvigne, he whispered a few words. The latter, at the window, signaled Girard to come up. Meeting him on the landing, he gave orders:

"Take all the men you have and surround the Gai-Moulin. Nobody's to leave. On the other hand, let anyone go in who wants to."

Then he returned to the room, where Adèle's white bedspread looked as fresh as whipped cream.

Victor was recovering his composure, and there was something about him that showed he could give trouble yet. His head could have served as a model for any cartoonist drawing a waiter: drooping features, large red-rimmed eyes, a bald head that should have been half-concealed by the thin graying hair that was usually carefully brushed over from one side to the other, but which had been ruffled thoroughly in the struggle.

His body was twisted sideways, as though to present a smaller target to Delvigne's gun. It was impossible to guess what was going on behind his shifty eyes.

"This isn't the first time you've been arrested, is it?" asked Maigret, but it sounded more like a statement than a question.

He was sure of it. It was written all over the man. Victor looked as though he was summoning all his resources to meet a situation long dreaded.

"I don't know what you mean," he answered suavely. "Adèle asked me to drop in and get something for her."

"Her lipstick, no doubt!"

"Finding someone here in the dark, I naturally took him for a burglar."

"And you went for him. Most public-spirited of you! . . . Keep those hands up, if you don't mind."

The raised arms were becoming limp. The boy's hands were trembling. He tried to wipe his forehead on one sleeve without lowering his arm.

"And you, young man? What did Adèle send *you* to get?"

René's teeth were chattering. He couldn't utter a word.

"Keep your eye on them, will you, Delvigne?" And with that, Maigret turned to inspect the room.

On the bedside table were signs of a meal—a plate with the remains of a cutlet, scattered crumbs, a glass, a half-consumed bottle of beer. He looked under the bed, shrugged, and opened the door of the wardrobe. It contained nothing but dresses, night things, and shoes with worn-down heels.

But all at once he noticed a chair that appeared to have been placed on purpose by the wardrobe. He climbed on it, felt on top of the wardrobe, and brought down a black leather briefcase.

"Aha!" he said. "This looks to me like Adèle's lipstick! Am I right, Victor?"

"I don't know what you mean."

"Isn't this what you came to get?"

"I've never seen it before."

"We'll find out about that. . . . And you, Delfosse?"

"I . . . I swear . . ."

Forgetting all about the gun pointed at him, he dived head first onto the bed and burst into a violent fit of sobbing.

There was no point in putting further questions to him. Maigret turned back to Victor.

"Well, my friend? Isn't there anything you'd like to say? . . . Won't you tell me what you and this young man were fighting about?"

He cleared the bedside table, putting the dirty plate and the beer bottle on the floor. In their place he put the briefcase and started examining its contents.

"These papers are hardly for us to deal with, Delvigne. You'll have to hand them over to the military authorities. . . . Look at this, for instance. Drawings of a new machine gun manufactured by Fabrique Nationale de Herstal. . . . As for this, it looks amazingly like a plan of the reconstruction of a fort. . . . Hmm . . . Letters in code. That'll be a specialist's job. . . ."

The remains of a fire were still flickering in the grate. And, without a second's warning, Victor darted forward and grabbed the papers Maigret was studying.

But the latter was not caught napping. Before Delvigne could make up his mind whether to use his gun, a heavy fist had struck the waiter full in the face.

Victor reeled, and the papers, instead of being thrown into the fire, were scattered over the floor.

René, not oblivious of what was happening, thought he'd take advantage of the confusion. He made a rush for the door, only to be stopped by Delvigne before he was halfway across the room.

"Well, my friend," Maigret began again.

"I have nothing to say," snarled Victor, who was holding a hand to his rapidly reddening cheek.

"Nothing to say!"

"Except that I didn't kill Graphopoulos."

"That's all?"

"You beast! . . . My lawyer will . . ."

"Dear me! So you already have a lawyer."

Meanwhile, Delvigne had been scrutinizing René. Following the boy's glance, he looked up at the wardrobe.

"I think there's something up there still."

"It's more than possible," answered Maigret, climbing onto the chair once more.

He groped for some time before finally lowering his hand, which was now holding a blue leather wallet.

"The Greek's," he said. "French money . . . Thirty thousand-franc notes . . . A few papers . . . Wait a minute!"

He studied a half-sheet of paper, with the letterhead GAI-MOULIN, RUE DU POT D'OR. Beneath it was a plan of the ground floor, and a handwritten note:

No one sleeps in the building.

It was the handwriting of those last few words that arrested Maigret's attention. He stopped, thoughtfully, and gathered up the papers lying on the floor, looking at each in turn, until he found the one he wanted: a letter in code.

"I think I've seen that writing before," he muttered. "One, two, three . . . nine, ten, eleven, twelve . . . Twelve letters. Might stand for Graphopoulos. . . ."

Steps could be heard coming up the stairs. Then a timid knock on the door. When Delvigne opened it, Girard came in and shut the door again behind him.

"Well?"

"The Gai-Moulin is surrounded. A few minutes ago Monsieur Delfosse arrived, asking for his son. He had a few words with Adèle, and then left. I guessed he'd be coming here and thought I'd better let him, and keep track of him myself. As soon as I was sure he was coming here, I nipped ahead to arrive first. . . . Here he is."

Indeed, someone could be heard tripping over a tear in the linoleum and groping in the dark for the door. Finally he knocked.

This time it was Maigret who opened the door. He bowed to the silver-haired man, who stared back haughtily.

"Is my son . . . ?" he began; then, catching sight of René's pitiful figure, he snapped his fingers and rapped out: "Come! We're going home."

The stage was set for a thoroughly sordid scene. René was back on the bed now, his teeth chattering worse than before. Clutching the bedspread, he huddled there, his panic-stricken eyes flitting from one to the other.

Maigret intervened:

"One moment, Monsieur Delfosse! . . . Perhaps you'll take a seat."

Monsieur Delfosse examined the room contemptuously.

"Who are *you*?"

"Never mind that. Inspector Delvigne will explain who I am in due course. . . . When your son arrived home today, did you give him a bad time?"

"I locked him in his room, and told him I would consider what was to be done with him."

"And what did you decide to do with him?"

"I haven't yet made up my mind. I'm thinking of sending him abroad, to work in a bank or in some business. It's high time he learned something about life."

"No, Monsieur Delfosse."

"What do you mean?"

"I mean this: it's not *high time;* it's *too late*. . . . On Wednesday night, your son killed Ephraim Graphopoulos and robbed him of his wallet."

Maigret side-stepped the gold-knobbed stick that was aimed at his head. With a sharp jerk, he wrenched it out of Monsieur Delfosse's hand, twisting the latter's wrist so painfully that the man gasped.

Calmly examining the stick and weighing it in his hand, he went on:

"And I am almost certain this is what he killed him with."

René's face twitched. His mouth opened, but no sound came. Racked by fear, he was nothing now but a pathetic bundle of nerves.

His father, however, did not yet haul down his flag.

"You'll have to answer for this amazing accusation," he said. Then, turning to Delvigne: "And you,

Inspector, you can count on my taking the matter up with my friend the public prosecutor."

"Bring Adèle here," Maigret said to Girard, "and Génaro too. Quick as you can. Take a taxi."

"I think . . ." Delvigne began nervously.

"Yes, yes. That's all right . . ." answered Maigret, in much the same voice one uses to soothe a child. And with that, he started pacing.

For seven minutes there was no other movement in the room. Only Maigret striding ponderously up and down, up and down.

A car pulled up outside, and soon there were steps on the stairs, and Génaro's voice, protesting:

"It'll be some time before you hear the last of this! We were doing such good business; so many people were coming. It's unheard of! As if we didn't have the whole day to answer your questions, you have to choose a time like this! . . ."

As he entered the room, his eyes sought Victor's inquiringly. The waiter put things in a nutshell:

"It's over," he said simply.

Adèle contemplated her room fatalistically: pursed lips, hanging arms, drooping shoulders.

"Just stick to the point, Adèle, and answer my questions. . . . Did Graphopoulos, in the course of the evening, ask you to join him in his room?"

"I didn't go."

"Then he did ask you. And that means he told you he was staying at the Hotel Moderne, in Room 18. . . ."

She hung her head.

"What's more, from where they were sitting, Chabot and Delfosse could easily have heard. What time was it when Delfosse arrived here?"

154

"I . . ."

"What time was it?"

"Five o'clock, maybe. I was asleep."

"What did he tell you?"

"He wanted me to run away with him. He said something about a ship to America. Said he had plenty of money."

"You refused?"

"I didn't consider it at all. For one thing, I was too sleepy. I told him he could share the bed, but he said he hadn't come for that. He seemed a little frantic, so I asked him if he'd done something."

"What did he say to that?"

"He asked me to hide a wallet. I told him to throw it up there. . . ."

"Along with the briefcase?"

She sighed and shrugged, as much as to say:

"How did I know about that?"

Monsieur Delfosse threw a defiant look around.

"What I'd like to know . . ." he began.

"You'll soon know everything," answered Maigret. "Give me one minute."

It was to light his pipe.

11

Room 18

"The story begins in Paris, where Graphopoulos first asks for police protection and then tries to shake it off. As I told you this morning, Delvigne, there were features of this case that made me think of spies and criminal organizations."

Maigret looked down at the black leather briefcase on Adèle's bedside table.

"I wasn't far wrong. This was an espionage case at the start, though in the middle it shifted to other ground. . . .

"Graphopoulos is rich. Like many rich people, he is bored; and, like many bored people, he craves excitement. In the course of his travels he must have run into some secret agent. That sets him dreaming. He too wants to lead a life of mystery and danger. Secret agent! Two words that have turned the head of many a fool before now. . . .

"They think the job consists of . . . but never mind that. . . . The Greek is set on the idea, and he tries to persuade his new acquaintance to introduce him to the world of espionage. The agent does not refuse. Graphopoulos is rich and knows his way around Europe. Excellent qualifications—as far as they go.

"Only, there are other qualifications, more essential ones: nerve and discretion. Does Graphopoulos possess them? That has to be found out.

"So he's given a trial job. He's told to go to Liège and steal some documents that are in a certain nightclub. The job is, of course, fake, simply a test of the candidate's mettle. If he goes to the police, and the Gai-Moulin is raided, no documents of any kind will be found there.

"But that's not to say the place isn't a haunt of spies. It is. Moreover, they belong to the organization the Greek wants to enter. Naturally, they're informed of his mission and asked to report on the way he acquits himself.

"To break into a place and steal! Graphopoulos is brought up, with a jolt, against the reality of the business. He'd seen it in quite a different and much rosier light—seen himself conducting secret negotiations with statesmen and ambassadors, perhaps even kings. Now suddenly the bottom falls out of this romance, and he's scared to death.

"He doesn't dare refuse. But, by getting himself shadowed, he provides himself with an excellent excuse. He can go to his boss and say: 'The police are after me, following me day and night. I'm afraid the job's off. . . .'

"And it's not difficult to imagine the answer:

" 'Get on with it!'

"His maneuver hasn't worked. In fact, he's worse off, since he now has to rid himself of the police. He reserves a plane seat for London, but at the last minute drives to the Gare du Nord and buys a ticket for Berlin, but he jumps out hastily at the Gare des Guillemins when the train stops here.

"I travel with him. Does he recognize me? I really can't say. But if he does, he is more frightened of the organization than of me. . . .

"So there he is at the Gai-Moulin, determined to go through with the job. A dancer comes to his table, and he invites her to his room: 18 at the Hotel Moderne. After all, there's no reason business should exclude pleasure; and excitement is a spur to sensuality. Besides, he doesn't want to be alone. . . . To win Adèle's favor, he gives her his gold cigarette case, which she had admired.

"He looks around nervously, but quite oblivious of the fact that Génaro is watching him. When Victor serves his champagne, it never occurs to him that the waiter is *one of them*, that behind his professional servility he too is watching, sardonically. . . .

"Thus far it's all about spies. By the merest chance, however, someone else has overheard what the Greek said to Adèle:

" 'Hotel Moderne . . . Room 18.'

"And that opens a new chapter. . . ."

Maigret turned to Monsieur Delfosse and addressed him personally:

"I must ask you to excuse me if I bring you into the story. . . . You're rich. You have a wife and a son, but that doesn't prevent your having a mistress. You

158

lead a life of self-indulgence, without giving a thought to the fact that your son, who's none too sound, in either health or character, is bound to follow your example to the best of his ability. . . .

"To the best of his ability—that's just the trouble. His means are limited. He's accustomed to seeing money squandered all around him, while he himself is given too much, yet at the same time too little. Enough to let him taste a life of pleasure, not enough to let him live it properly. For years he's been stealing money from you when he needs it—except when he robs his uncle for a change.

"When you're away, he drives your car and swaggers around with your gold-knobbed stick. In fact, a more typical case of a badly brought-up boy going to the dogs would be hard to find. . . . It's no use protesting. It's the truth—as you'll see.

"He needs a friend—I might almost say an accomplice. So he ropes in young Chabot. And one day when they're desperate, owing money all over the place, they decide to take a crack at the till of the Gai-Moulin.

"So there were two separate performances on the program that night! . . . Following their plan, the two boys hid on the cellar steps, after pretending to leave. Did Génaro know they were there? I don't know, but I wouldn't be surprised. He was certainly keeping his eyes open that night.

"And Génaro's sharp—you can be sure of that. The very model of a competent secret agent. He pays his way, never gets into trouble, and, to keep on the right side of the police, he's always ready to act as informer if he knows of anybody else up to something.

159

"Just what the sequence of events was isn't clear. Like Delfosse and Chabot, did the Greek find a hiding place in the Gai-Moulin? Or did he leave, as Victor and Génaro make out? It's equally possible either way. He may easily have been supplied with a key to the place. . . . But that doesn't matter. What's certain is that he was in the nightclub shortly after it closed.

"There he is, primed with champagne, groping about in the dark for documents that don't exist. But he's hardly set to work, when the door at the back of the room opens and the boys creep in. He can't see them or guess who they are. If he was scared before, he's now petrified.

"He doesn't have the courage to tackle them. On the other hand, he knows he's bound to be seen, because he hears Chabot ask Delfosse for a light. The only thing he can think to do is lie down and pretend to be dead.

"The boys have no more courage than he does, and the sight of him lying on the floor routs them completely."

In Adèle's room no one moved. It even seemed that no one was breathing. Almost every face bore signs of strained attention. Quietly, placidly, Maigret went on:

"The Greek presumably continues his fruitless search. The boys go have some mussels and fried potatoes, after which they separate at the Delfosses' house. Chabot goes home to bed, thinking his friend is doing the same. . . . But he isn't. . . .

"Hotel Moderne. Room 18. . . .

"The words ring in René's ears. He needs money.

160

It's become an obsession with him. And the Greek must be rich. What could be easier than to have a look in a dead man's room? The key will no doubt be hanging in the hall.

"He's had time to recover his self-confidence. Besides, this is child's play compared to the job they had planned, which even so would have gone off perfectly if it hadn't been for that corpse. . . .

"At the hotel, the porter is too sleepy to check him. The key is on the board, and up he goes. Room 18 is bare. Nothing lying around. Nothing to lay his hands on, unless it's in the Greek's suitcase. . . . But he has no time to open it.

"Graphopoulos has reached the hotel only a few steps behind him. Not finding his key on the board, he rushes upstairs and bursts in.

"Picture the scene from the boy's point of view. The dead man come to life! He's terrified out of his wits. Can you wonder if he loses his head completely and lashes out . . .

"With this . . . ?"

Once more Maigret weighed the gold-knobbed stick in his hand.

"He has, however, sufficient presence of mind for one thing: he takes the Greek's wallet with him. Such a sum of money has never been in his hands before. With that much, he can toy with the idea of going to America with Adèle.

"But Adèle, as she says herself, doesn't take to the idea. She's too sleepy! When he asks her to let him leave the stolen wallet here, she's too sleepy to think of any other place for it than *the* hiding place, the one

Génaro and Victor are in the habit of using when, from time to time, they want a safe place for compromising papers.

"So he throws the thing up there, after removing from it all the Belgian money. He thinks the French money is too dangerous.

"The account he reads in the next day's papers is nothing short of bewildering. For I've taken a hand in things myself, and the body he left in Room 18 is discovered on a public lawn, in a basket. He lives in perpetual fear now. He finds Chabot, and to explain the money, he says he stole it from his uncle's shop.

"On second thought, he decides that even this money is too dangerous to keep. Apparently he's frightened of doing anything with it himself . . . but it's more than that, worse than that. After all, he has plenty of opportunity to get rid of the stuff unnoticed. In his own home, for instance.

"No. It isn't merely fear, but also some obscure desire to involve his friend. An odd friendship that, if it can be called one at all. I'm certain that he's always borne Chabot a grudge. Degenerate that he is, he's intelligent enough to resent all that's clean and decent. Chabot's weak, yes, but at bottom he's a decent boy.

"Well, we can't go into that now. The point is that he *does* get Chabot involved, by giving him the money to flush down the toilet at the Gai-Moulin.

"In the meantime, Génaro—no less puzzled than anyone by the Greek's death—has been to the police, to square himself. He has put them on the track of Delfosse and Chabot, with the result that the latter does not return from the lavatory. Becoming more and more uneasy, Delfosse finally goes to see what's happened. No sign of him. . . .

"And Delfosse spends the rest of the evening drowning himself in drink. . . .

"In the morning he wakes up in this room. His situation seems desperate when he sees a policeman walking up and down outside. He doesn't dare touch the French money that's lying on top of the wardrobe. The Belgian money's been disposed of. So he takes Adèle's, and sneaks out by the back way.

"He makes for the station, but he's too upset to work out any consistent plan. . . . Ask Inspector Delvigne where the police look for criminals of his type—and where they find them nine times out of ten. In houses of ill repute. They need drink, noise, women. . . .

"So, instead of going to the station, Delfosse ends up in a bar nearby. He tries to pick up the waitress, and when she declines, he hauls girls in from the street. He drinks himself silly and stands round after round for all comers, squandering the money meant for his escape. He doesn't care. He's out of control.

"Next morning, when he's brought to the Sûreté, he lies, wildly, idiotically, hopelessly, for the sake of lying, like a child. He's ready to say anything, invent the most improbable details. . . .

"Then suddenly the scene changes. He's told the murderer has been arrested—that's me—and later learns that I've committed suicide.

"After hopelessness, bewilderment again . . . Does he really believe the danger's over, or does he think he has merely been given a breathing space? Does he come for the money because he now feels free to use it, or does he come to destroy it, the only material evidence of his guilt? I daresay he'd be hard put to answer those questions.

"In any case, he comes. . . .

"We stage this little comedy to induce the murderer to show his hand. He does so, and in the process shows everybody else's. To retrieve the Greek's money, he must have the key to this room. Adèle gives it to him.

"But his back's no sooner turned than Victor questions her, and she tells him about the wallet. To his horror, he learns that it's been sharing a hiding place with their precious papers, and he dashes off to save them. If Delfosse gets hold of them . . . !

"Victor arrives in time. . . . But so do we. . . ."

Slowly Maigret looked around at his audience, his eyes finally resting on Adèle.

"How long has Génaro enjoyed the use of your room for hiding compromising documents?"

It was with resignation, almost indifference, that Adèle shrugged weakly, like a woman who's known all along that someday it would all come out.

"For years," she answered. "He brought me with him from Paris, where I was down and out."

"Is that right, Génaro?"

"I'll answer questions in the presence of my lawyer."

"Oh! So you have a lawyer too!"

Monsieur Delfosse was staring silently at the gold knob of his stick, the stick that had cost Graphopoulos his life. In a hollow voice he said:

"My son's not responsible for his actions."

"I know."

The manufacturer looked anxiously into the stolid Frenchman's eyes.

"You . . . ?"

"Yes, I know," Maigret said in a curt, businesslike tone: "Your lawyer will have no difficulty proving him insane."

Three months later, in his apartment on Boulevard Richard-Lenoir, Maigret was looking through his mail.

"Anything interesting?" asked Madame Maigret as she vigorously shook a rug out the window.

"A card from your sister."

"What does she say?"

"I'm not quite sure. It's rather cryptic. Sounds as though she's expecting another baby."

"Another!"

"And a letter from Belgium . . . with a photograph . . ."

"Who?"

Maigret stared at the snapshot of a narrow-shouldered young man in the uniform of some colonial service, standing in front of the funnel of a ship.

"A wretched boy who got in trouble. I helped to get him out."

Thoughtfully Maigret unfolded the letter, which was written in a clerk's neat hand:

. . . and I am taking the liberty of sending you a photograph of my son, who sailed from Antwerp this

week on the Elisabethville, *bound for the Congo.*
Roughing it in the Colonies will soon make a man
of him. . . .

In carefully turned phrases, Monsieur Chabot
went on to express his gratitude, and a half-humorous,
half-embarrassed look spread over the inspector's
heavy features.